Blueprints for

Better Worlds

Also by Tenea D. Johnson

R/evolution, Book One of the Revolution Series
Evolution, Book Two of the Revolution Series
Smoketown
Starting Friction

Blueprints for Better Worlds

Tenea D. Johnson

counterpoise (koun´tər poiz´), n., v.: both a
balancing force and the equilibrium it creates—books and
compositions, stories to music, timeless records.

counterpoise records
PO Box 1728
St. Petersburg, Fl 33731

ISBN: 978-1-7339797-3-3

Cover Art by Reid Jenkins.
Cover Design by Brianna Kole.

Which world are you living in? Might it be better? May you make it so.

CONTENTS

ACKNOWLEDGMENTS

Thank you to all the little lights leading me home.

BEAST — 2

Jak and Clem made their first sun out of reflectors and foil insulation pulled from the wrecked copters that littered the Gog. All those copters had crashed in unison, right along with shuttles and lifts, rockets and airliners all over North America. But for a few intact blades and the fuselage of one that looked like it hadn't got 10 feet off the ground, in the Gog, you couldn't tell they'd been helicopters. But everyone, everywhere, had seen the footage.

It'd happened long before either Jak or Clem was born, before the first alien contact, before the sea swallowed all but the world's peaks. But not before pollution's haze dimmed the sky.

The beat up bit of Arkansas where they lived still got streaks of blue sky but in most places, strong, natural light became a thing to long for, and for the girls, one to harness.

To Jak and Clem, the Gog's ruins were more treasure than tragedy.

They could create possibilities with those ruins, make progress, fix some of the broken they'd been born to.

They built their sun to bounce light into the deepest corners of Clem's tenement. That sun's light ran through the big adobe warren of three hundred, past the hydroponic garden in the basement, straight down to the subbasement where Clem's grandmother fed the kiln that fired the pots she traded for her and Clem's food.

Everything was work here. That is until the spring Clem met Jak and the Gog became more than the edge of a boneyard.

Still, the two of them built the best parts of it, two wild-headed girls barely into their teens.

So when a gale scattered their sun into oblivion, plunging Clem's grandmother, Triz, and the tenements' subfloor farmers back into the dark, Grand called on the girls to make another.

She called as the two of them lay face up, head to head, on a patch of grass surrounded by a sea of thin dirt that lay just outside of the tenement's shadow. Grand's voice cut though the orange murk of dusk, and their conversation.

Respirators covered the bottom half of their faces, but even those didn't hinder their talk. The girls paused when Grand called, then went on sharing their dreams of space—the regular meals and clean water, the better life that beckoned them offworld. But also the yawning spaces between ships and what prizes they might find there.

They spoke of flying away in the newmoon starfarer, of the end of gravity, and their best breaths released into a capsule that could clean them so they wouldn't come hacking back every time their respirators clogged.

Grand called again.

A third call without a response would get Clem chores enough to fill a whole day. Clem pinched either side of the clean cell on her respirator and yelled back, "Coming!"

She rolled over onto her stomach and peered down at Jak. Clem moved her head so her afro blocked out the warmth that could have hit Jak, made a face that said, "*So*" and cocked her head.

Jak had tried to convince her to loc her hair like Jak's but Clem preferred it grow out, not down, no matter how long it took to comb out. She didn't tell Jak she wouldn't be able to do this anymore if she did, but it figured somewhere in her decision.

"Coming?" Clem asked.

Jak looked past her friend to the edges of dark quickly approaching.

"I ought to get back. Gotta seal up before the cold comes," Jak replied.

"Your place has a seal?" Clem asked, one eyebrow arched. Curiosity about where exactly Jak lived flared every evening they parted, every time Clem watched Jak walk beyond the rubble walls that bordered the tenement's south side and disappear into the dark.

Jak flicked her gaze from the sky to Clem's face. Jak's respirator shifted a bit. Clem couldn't see behind it, but would bet she was smirking. Jak arched her eyebrow slightly, made a noncommittal noise and got up, careful not to clip Clem as she rose.

"Tell your Grand I said 'hello'," Jak replied.

*

Jak should have known that sun wouldn't survive the winds here. She'd figured in the effects of

3

heat and sand but hadn't adequately accounted for the velocity of the wind. The new sun would require a sturdier base and reflective pieces that would move with the gusts, not resist them.

She reached into a front pocket of her pants and removed the sketch she'd drawn last night. Jak preferred straight pants to the folds of fabric Clem sported. A bit of breeze stirring around her legs couldn't beat the ease straight pants gave an unexpected run. Quiet as these parts had been since she arrived, Jak believed in staying ready so she wouldn't have to get ready. That was the only lasting thing Mite ever said to her, but it had stuck when everything else fell away.

Jak's fingertips bumped along the rough, thick sheet as she opened the square of paper. After a quick look, she flipped it over to the list of materials, handed it over to Clem.

Clem shielded her eyes from a gust of sand and angled the list up, nodding as she read. As Clem walked over the small jagged rocks and bones underfoot, not quite buried in the sand, Jak watched her slow and stop, then scan the horizon. Jak followed her gaze to the eastern edges of the Gog where the swollen belly of a military cargo aircraft lay cracked open and filled with sand, all but its edges hidden from view. That part of the Gog might yield smaller pins and shanks they could use to hold the sun together. With few windbreaks, parts had scattered and broken down quicker, which made it easier to find the small bits without having to disassemble much, and if those parts could survive the initial impact and years of exposure here, they'd easily keep the new construction together.

Wind kicked up out of nothing and blew a wave of sand across her and Clem's feet and legs. Grudgingly Jak pulled her respirator off a loop in her pants and put it on just as Clem did the same. Jak inched her gaze west, trying to decide on the most efficient path to find what they required. She took the Gog in as she thought it over. Much as the phantom sun had bleached most of the Gog to one washed out shade of old, the place had an eerie beauty. The shades of brown and yellow often yielded bands of gold, both pale and rich, in the hills behind the tufts of grass and cacti. Hardy shrubs clung to the parched land, held in place by deep roots that found water far beneath the dust. Amongst the metal wrecks and bright white shards of bone there were boulders a coral color so deep it ran to red.

And at the outskirts of it all, stubborn trees stood their ground proving the Gog was only semi-arid.

Jak felt her feet slip further into the sand as she took a step, as if trying to pull her down into its rich and weary earth.

"Start in the Cut?" Jak asked, turning to Clem.

Clem nodded and fell in step beside her as they headed that direction.

Clem hummed a tune as they searched.

A shard of white sticking out of a dune caught Jak's attention, a jawbone by the looks of it. Back in Kentucky she'd met people who would have fought for that, seen a reliable weapon or hand trowel for scavenging. No one did that here. No grave robbers or makers. She'd met plenty on that long walk here. It'd been the only reason she stopped walking.

Part of her still wanted to hide the bone. She wondered if that was to save it from someone else or save it for herself. She looked over at Clem, moved the thought aside, focused on the task at hand.

For their new sun, she and Clem would fashion a spiral spine, bending it to the degrees that best bent. And they'd have to dig a base this time. That'd mean precious liniment rubbed on sore muscles tomorrow; so Jak would make the most of the use and dig the filtration lines for her pod as well. They wouldn't have to crush and prepare cement for the sun, but she'd brought a pulley from her pod to place anchor boulders around its main shaft.

They walked down a narrow path into the Cut. The Cut was made from a cleaving of two pieces of earth split into a V where fuel or rainwater had surged violently enough to tear away most of the earth in its path. That liquid was long gone, but the ravine and depression it created remained. There, parts pooled together as if they'd been dumped expressly for salvaging purposes. It'd been picked over more than the rest the Gog, but it could yield surprisingly useful bits.

As they came to the bottom of the depression Jak stepped around the dubiously green water that collected there, careful not to make a splash. The Gog and surrounding area contained precious pockets of freshwater, but this wasn't it. This water never moved and she'd seen more than one kangarat meet its end down here, barely able to make it a few hops before it keeled over and died a quick, shuddering death.

Clem pulled the folded fabric on her hips apart and reached in the left pocket there, removed a hand broom, hitched up her pants and knelt. Jak joined her with her industrial tweezers, a prize possession Mite had left behind along with a cracked tablet all those years before. Jak used the bent end to pick around a tangle of black and green cased wires and extract a long linchpin, then half a dozen others nearly as long. She mentally crossed them off the list. Working next to her, Clem unearthed three arm-lengths of thick-gauged wire. She looped it into a small circle that she hooked onto the back of the belt beneath her pant folds. The Cut was well worth the walk today.

In another hour they'd halved the list and straightened their stiff legs, ready to move on.

Just up the rise from the Cut, they stood and stared at the full span of the Gog just beneath them. It fanned out for as far the distant hills.

Even from this vantage point it didn't look like a Great Old Graveyard. Not even folks Grand's age called it that anymore. From here it was metal, fiberglass, twisted hunks of machine and broken bones, all of it burnished by the sorrowful wind that swept over the field of wrecks.

The debris stood half Jak's height in places though most lay scattered close to the ground. Because the main departure point for the shuttle ferries stood just a few miles north, dozens of copters converged here and here they'd stayed to bake and rot in the sand at the perimeter of the grassland. Jak had walked through the long runway of grass when she'd arrived here, the first place she wanted to stay since Mite left her in the attic to join a traveling group of thieves.

Jak remembered the feel of that thick of grass brushing her bare ankles as she walked and how it tickled as the grass petered down to a few tufts just a few feet from where she and Clem looked.

"What's left?" Clem asked Jak who walked a half step ahead.

"Mirrors. As many as we can find," Jak answered.

"So the Ramparts?"

"Yes, there should be some left in that dead spot near the rise."

"Parapet," Clem said.

"If you say so, wordblack," Jak responded.

"You're doing that on purpose."

"Doing what?" Jak said with a smirk.

Clem huffed, whispered that Jak knew the damn word under her breath.

As they dodged rusty, sharp edges, Jak slowed to match Clem's pace. She took a deep breath, content for the moment with the gentle breeze that entered the loose weave of her shirt and cooled the sweat under her arms, across her chest. Clem spoke.

"Think: To make it all the way here . . ." Clem swept her gaze out across the expanse and toward the rendezvous point ". . just to die in the dirt."

"They had a way out, " Jak said. "People in the cities, the towns, all the people like us or anyone with less than, how much did Grand say?, $4 million US, they were splite and fucked, every last one."

"Should have been," Clem said.

Jak nodded her head. Indeed. Who could have guessed the Womazu would materialize with the snow and give the last humans a fighting chance? She doubted anyone dreamed of microscopic aliens, prominent only in their ability halt the humans' panic.

*

After a long break and short nap in a rock face's shadow at midday, they finished assembly and moved the last anchoring boulder into place. Clem went down to Grand's den to check the light. Jak secured the rope and moved into the respite of an overhang, squinted into the haze. From here some days it looked like the sun was dying, though Jak knew it wasn't. It's just that so much haze now stood between it and them, and all the other folks pushed all the way out to the edges of habitability.

She'd seen images taken in other places and could scarcely believe it was the same world at the same time. Here the world could be as blurry as a buried memory.

Yet it intensified the sunsets. The whole world went the colors of extinct blooms. She couldn't help but appreciate that, especially on a day like today when something had been accomplished. She lived in that juxtaposition, just as much as anyplace else.

Clem came back smiling, a bag of tepary beans in hand, jerky in the other. Jak didn't bother to ask if it had worked.

"Imagine what we could make if there were more of us," Clem said as she tossed the jerky to her.

*

Jak headed home in half light, dragging a makeshift sled of salvage behind her. She kept her gaze on the sky and her head in the clouds.

It would return soon; she could feel it. You couldn't predict exact days, only probabilities by how much time had passed.

Regular as the phases of the Qxn moon (full once every two Earth years Jak knew), the newmoon starfarer returned. She'd grown up watching the huge interstellar ship, dark as a newmoon night, advance and recede as it orbited the dimming stars. Some folks said it broadcast coordinates; Mite's Mama even plugged some of them into the tablet before she gave it to Mite who'd let it slip from her hands while she dead-eyed the old woman and told her not to fill their heads with farmer's tales. Even back when Mite kept her hidden, Jak would look up at it from the hole in the attic roof and imagine where the starfarer had just gone and where it might next go. She dreamed of another version of herself looking through its windows out toward this peaceforsaken rock. From there did it seem a planet or a star?

Jak smiled to herself, kept moving toward the stand of trees that marked the periphery of her territory, or what she thought of as her territory. It belonged to the snakes really, but they'd come to a truce. They'd warm themselves out in the open here and not on her pod's ladder and she would use her slingshot on other game. She didn't much like snake though other meat could be hard to find. So it was a halfhearted sacrifice at best. Her stomach grumbled thinking of the tepary beans she'd seen Clem sneak into her bag.

Just before she crossed into the trees' shadows, she glanced back up. Tonight's sky held only the haze and the diffused light of distant galaxies. Shame that. So few lights out here she should have been able to see into the past and future, if only the air could clear. At the end of the grove, she picked up the bag, shoved the sled into a low dune by its thin edge until it disappeared. The wind might scrub her path from the sand, but the trees here blocked it and the thin dirt would show it.

Her pod had many strengths not least of all its hidden location. Clem could probably find it if she set her mind to it; she was clever and brave enough. But

10

she hadn't. Jak counted it amongst the reasons she searched the other girl out most days. After she finished the filter lines, tomorrow would be no different.

*

Late the next morning Clem waited for Jak near the sandy side of the trees. She'd walked through a full beam of sunlight when she went to fetch Grand's newest pitcher from the kiln. She couldn't wait to tell Jak.

She saw her round a stand of trees halfway to her.

"This one's twice as good as the last! Maybe three times. Other folks are asking for one," Clem shouted.

"You can't throw together two or three suns in a day," Jak teased, now only steps away.

"I'm serious, Jak."

"As am I. Besides we have other things to do today."

"What's that?" Clem asked.

"I was thinking we might—" Jak stopped, chewed a bit on her bottom lip, looked just above Clem's head, thinking. She clenched her jaw.

"You told me about the other stuff, those peddlers and what happened in Kentucky," Clem said gently, trying to loosen that jaw.

Jak looked back down into Clem's eyes. Jak's expression softened.

"I met you before I knew any better," Jak said.

"That was *four months* ago." Clem replied. Jak's eyebrows popped up.

"I was younger then," she responded slyly, backing away from her. *Good*, she could tell Jak felt

11

better. Clem watched as Jak turned around, took a few swift steps away.

"Coming?" Jak asked. Clem cursed softly, shook her head, and quickly caught up.

After the stand of trees where they usually parted, the further trees stood low to the ground. Dark bark covered the thin branches sprawling in every direction to create a kind of canopy for each one, each flat at the bottom as if some short, thick beast ran rampant and knocked them all into submission or the trees had learned to keep their branches far from the ground. Beyond them a rock formation of jagged individual pieces ten times her or Jak's height covered a hill. A narrow path cut through them. As they walked, Clem noted how much green still popped up in the orange and reddish crags—a bush here, a tuft of grass there. The path ended at a wall of rock, smooth as it was steep, not a hand or foothold in sight. Jak pointed at a crevice of space at the bottom.

"Through there," Jak said. Clem's face must have reflected her thoughts. Jak took a step closer.

"It's safe . . . enough. I do it every day."

Clem relented.

They crawled flat on their bellies and emerged in a plot of sunlight, warm and hidden by the surrounding rock. Jak popped up to standing. Clem unfolded her body and joined her friend, looked the direction of Jak's gaze.

Clem's breath caught. She squinted, walked slowly up to Jak's place. She wondered at the design of things for the first time since her mother passed.

It was perfect, Jak's place. Virtually flawless. Sure the bottom panel had taken most of the impact, but those Robins were built to take a beating, and it was just a quarter panel, common as landing skids.

The booster tips still had points. It even looked like Jak or the wind had sanded them to fine, optimum shape.

"I didn't tell you it was a pod 'cause—," Jak began. Clem placed her hand on Jak's shoulder, gaze still locked on the pod as she spoke.

"In that," she turned to Jak, "we can make it to the ship."

*

That day, Clem had said it with such certainty that the puff of belief caught fire and Jak'd huddled round it, pulled the thin hope closer.

Now Jak wasn't so sure. She had been after they found three candidate quarter panels and when Grand traded for a quarter roll of emery cloth 'cause the seller couldn't see anything but the licorice fern in her bowl, and especially the morning Clem had muscled the last bolt down, singing so happily that Jak joined in.

Now a tempest beat at what they built, and Jak couldn't even reach it much less protect it.

Inside the cave where she sheltered it sounded as if all the fire-feeding air in hell had broken free and now ripped through the world. Jak had beat the sandstorm to this clutch of caves, but she couldn't make it the pod. Her bounty of skinned kangarat lay in her bag. She wanted to roast and eat it, but dared not attract something worse from the inner reaches of this place. The sound of the storm echoed, bouncing against the rock walls.

She waited, listening for the break that would mean she could venture out. As the moments crawled past she contemplated how long she might be stuck, pulled a piece of jerky from a corner of her inner shirt pocket to calm her grumbling stomach.

On the fourth day the gale died.

She woke to silence. Jak closed her eyes and listened again, then shoved her feet in her boots, put her respirator on and hurried outside. For a moment the sun blinded her and she blinked back the bright. Raising her palm to her forehead, she squinted, waiting. Then she jogged to the pod and scurried on her belly to see what was left.

Her pants caught and ripped against a shiv of bone. She stopped herself, slowed her breathing and movement. She had to grab hold, lest an injury or infection end what hadn't yet begun. She closed her eyes and gingerly moved her hand back around her and into the thin crevice whose contents caught her, grabbed the smaller bit of fabric she'd have to sacrifice and pulled. Unhooked, she wriggled the rest of the way out, gaze searching up and around to see over the rocks.

It had survived.

She had two long nights and a day's work ahead of her, but that was all. As she watched sand drip from the pod's apron, she exhaled, closed her eyes with relief, then got to work.

Jak set into the work with purpose, resting only when her back demanded to be stretched out from her stooped position on the ground or food and facilities required.

When Clem showed up it went faster than she'd calculated.

*

Two more parts—a replacement and a backup —and they'd be done.

They started off down Moon Ridge, a thick vein of destruction and dust pushed into existence by the impact of a B2700 scalping the airfield as it flew half a mile 100 feet from the ground before it finally smashed into it. No one who'd seen the footage quite understood why something so large had glided for so long before it finally succumbed to gravity. Jak searched until she found the answer, combing through every aeronautic site and image bank she could access on the tablet. But it took Clem to explain the tiny mechanics behind it. It'd been their first conversation when they met on this ridge. To Jak and Clem the wrecks meant parts; just about all of them useful. It all depended on the use. Not unlike the histories of why and what had happened here. One thing Clem and Jak knew was undisputed: The plane had been brand new, top of the line. Unfortunately, they couldn't salvage anything from that crash because the mountain had broken off there. You could peer over the ledge if you wanted to get your heart beating, but any metal, bits, boards, and hardware had long ago fallen into the chasm where the mountain ended. Years ago, before Jak had come, Clem crawled out toward the drop but no longer had such an inclination. Once on the edge of nothingness was enough.

Moon Ridge also intermittently held thin streams. A small web of them ran through today.

As Clem and Jak rounded Moon Ridge something glittered in the bright sunlight. Sometimes the sand and wind rubbed the metal until it gleamed. It helped you avoid cutting yourself as you crossed the debris field, but mostly it just blinded you at inopportune moments. From the ridges overhead the whole place twinkled. Lovely in a way that didn't seem possible from any other angle. Down here amongst the wreckage it was easy to forget any secret magical properties beyond how the parts might aid a solar cell repair or serve a desalination unit. But Clem could understand why some old folks only came out to pay their respects on full moons. She'd seen it plenty when was small and Grand brought her. What with the black of the desert and twinkling of the moon amongst shrapnel one could feel as if they'd been transported to the stars.

This afternoon had no such glamour, just heat and stiff gusts that pushed the sand to cover and uncover a thousand treasures. Today Clem had a particular treasure in mind.

Her check of the pod yielded only one crucial part missing, a sealed stem circuit, and she'd bet a porcelain pot that one could be found somewhere in this section of the Gog. Pods dotted this stretch all the way up to the Cat's Rise. Rich folks who weren't quite rich enough to buy themselves a seat on a military transport or pay the ransom to charter a copter had launched from this area. That generation of pods were designed to be foolproof. They didn't handle well but they came with instructions, adequate automation, and could shoot 500 lbs into the exosphere without incinerating whoever was inside (fuel line composition and atmospheric conditions notwithstanding).

Clem gathered her skirts and crossed a narrow stream. Jak joined her, knelt and plunged her hand in to the water where the piece glittered just below the surface. She cocked her head as she examined it, then handed it to Clem.

Promising. She'd have a better idea once she laid it out to dry and swabbed it clean, but it was certainly worth keeping. She opened the side fold of her pants and dropped it into the large pouch there, gathered the fabric to hide the items underneath.

"Another. Let's find another," Clem said.

They set off to the west, as always. On the way back home they'd find a spot to watch the horizon shift through colors to darkness. When they did, Jack finally asked.

"What about Grand?"

"Grand loves me enough to let me go. Just like my mother."

Jak didn't say more. Clem was glad of it. After, as they parted, each had a piece to take and prepare. Tomorrow they'd see how well they fit the pod.

*

Her bag filled with three fillets of fresh kangarat and what she hoped was a newly pristine sealed stem circuit, Jak was on her way to Clem and Grand's. Her mind was on other things. She'd need to make a list of
—

Steps from the tenement, Jak stumbled as she stopped—she knew that sound, that susurrus in the sky—and craned her neck up.

It slid slowly into place, gliding through clouds until it filled her vision, knocking everything else out of focus.

It slid into view quiet and welcome as a kiss.

She heard steps crunch in the sand, tore her gaze away.

Clem stared up as she walked toward her, glancing down every few steps until she'd made it to Jak's side. Their shoulders touched.

"Let's get your filthy beast cleaned up," Clem said.

Jak smiled at the joke, the joy that dared show itself, coaxed by possibility.

*

Though she'd memorized its contents days ago, Clem rubbed the instruction manual with one thumb as she held it. She found the sequence odd, but not impossible—square, trapezoid, a haiku, and a dog star. That's how she remembered the button and switch locations because of the slight modification they'd had to make to the dampening jets. The pods were designed for consumers to operate she kept reminding herself and not necessarily bright ones, just rich. She and Clem only had to change two things, the wiring for the jets and the heat panels. She felt sure she'd followed the wiring diagram for the jets exactly and the panels would buckle or they wouldn't. She added as many layers as she knew wouldn't skew the trajectory the closest coordinates in Jak's tablet, then contemplated adding another thin layer until Jak made her stop.

All the panel lights were illuminated; a soft current of arid air flowed from the vents. Everything seemed to be in working order she assured herself.

Jak watched her calmly. Clem hoped some of her confidence would rub off. When Jak reached out and placed a hand on her leg, gave her a rare sweet smile, it did.

Clem nodded, exhaled and reached for the first corner of the square. At the dog star she exhaled a long shout she didn't know was coming.

Instantly, rumbling began beneath them and roared in their ears. Beast fought against the ground, each bit of motion a miracle until all its power gathered and pushed them an inch, a foot, and then up into the air.

Then every thought left her head and she was lifted.

*

Beast had no windows, just a framed 15-ply square of clear reinforced plex at their feet. So they could see each other, and what they left behind, but nothing else. As they moved up, Jak thought death must be that way.

The temperature inside creeped higher.

Something screeched on the outside of the pod. A panel buckling? She locked gazes with Clem.

They both knew what could happen. She'd made her peace with it and knew Clem must have too. Resolution would break their fall. Of the body or spirit remained to be seen.

Everything vibrated: her teeth to her bones, every panel and light in the pod. Or perhaps it just seemed to be that way because Jak shook so violently. Clem shook next to her. Clem's hand made a vice on her shoulder, a comforting pressure while the rest of the world gave way.

Beneath, they watched their world slip away— the crags and tenement, the dunes of the Gog, the place they'd carved out for themselves.

It all disappeared. Then there was only the brown haze and, gift!, a snippet of sun, hot and golden, as the pod's angle showed what all their days had been missing.

Determination was a force, but like many such forces it sometimes lacked the ability to calibrate.

The view beneath them changed.

They saw the starfarer's big black doors crack open, ready to receive them.

The pod rocketed on.

At their feet, Jak saw a fountain of smoke surging into the blue. It sputtered for a second and gray cleared into a blue she'd only seen in polished quartz and Grand's bowls but never in the sky. That glimpse of clarity made her blink. So it took her a second to understand the black that replaced it, to understand she was starting at space. The smoke returned then, each molecule of it pushing them further into the abyss.

Fuck, she thought. Not a bit of panic, just a sharp sweet sadness. Clem had come for *this*?

The thought consumed her. So much so that she almost didn't feel the pod slowing, the force pulling them back.

"What is that?! Jak! What is that?" Clem shouted.

At their feet, night rippled. But it had been day, they'd left during the day.

Jak stopped, stunned. She recognized the newmoon wing of the starfarer as it floated past their feet. Its doors opened and the pod was pulled inside, gently settled on a slate gray floor, ending what little view they had. They were blind now, and tucked inside an alien ship. The sound of air rushing in filled Beast. Jak felt her lungs expand to a point until then unknown. Her head swam with alertness. The air was so fresh it had a taste. She gulped it in.

*

A woman's voice, amplified and tinny, called from outside the pod.

Jambo
Konichiwa
Hola
Hello

The pod door cracked open. A strange smell, sweet and lovely, flooded in. Clem looked at Jak, pushed the door open as Jak hurried to stop her. Jak saw something through the crack, stepped aside as Clem pushed.

It wasn't a woman. Perhaps still female but not human. This person was taller, had translucent skin with light that danced beneath so that her/its/the entire body seemed to glow. There was rhythm to it, like the flow of one's breath. Clem wondered if this person, 'person' probably wasn't even right, if she breathed. She smiled at her, that was definitely a smile, and began the litany of greetings again, only stopped when Clem answered.

"Hello."

"Words, then, yes let's use words," the female person said.

"Is there another way?" Jak asked.

Clem's mind filled with information, but mostly an invitation. They could stay. Anyone who reached the ship had a choice. It was their law. They had seen what happened to Earth's evacuees.

Clem marveled. But briefly. She saw the beauty of it, what she and Jak had found, but when she did more than listen and look at what had been offered, she could only think of what was lost and might still be found.

Clem's chest ached. It now always would she knew. It wasn't a choice between Grand or Jak. Much as she loved them both, there was no contest. Nor did she fear space now that she'd touched it. She felt no yawning chasms or voids open up to invade her soul.

What she felt was responsible and just now she felt Jak, solid and warm as she turned and embraced her. Clem held her until to do so longer would cause more pain.

The female person moved away and waited at the threshold between this bay and the rest of the ship. Clem closed her eyes, for how long she did not know. She heard metal scrape metal and a soft whirring behind her. She didn't turn to the noise or say anything. She just cried quietly with Jak, the two of them standing on the deck of a dream they'd once shared.

With an exhalation, Clem released her, let her hands float up to Jak's shoulders, then just the fingertips brushing Jak's face as Clem stepped back and onto the deck of the small shuttle that hovered behind her. Her gaze never left Jak's. She tried to take in every detail of her. She knew she should; the little voice in her head told her so, but she couldn't look away from Jak's eyes. When the shuttle door slid to a close and she began her descent she closed them, didn't open them again until she heard the door open, heat pushed its way in and she felt the glare of the Gog beating at her lids.

Her first steps didn't bring her back to Grand or the lower levels. Instead she climbed Cat's Rise, the soft rock underneath the farthest lip and carved with the shard of a stone, her own design, this one for infinity, *Jak & Clem 4 Ever*.

*

Jak sat alone in the room they'd assigned her, blind to the beauty that surrounded her. She saw the sleek, shimmering surfaces and the provider ready to serve up whatever meal might meet her fancy. The immense metal shades that bordered the top perimeter of the room were drawn. The universe didn't interest her for the moment.

She could only think of Clem. Once Clem had decided, Jak knew she would not be moved. Not an inch or a light year, to the next world or back a single second to choose differently. They could both believe in a purpose, know how to bring it to being and do so. But there they parted.

It's not what Jak'd imagined, but it seemed to be the only way it worked. This more than the rest confounded her. Taught her the limits of anyone's designs.

Finally, fitfully, she opened the shades, tweaked the gravity, turned away and slept.

That first night, when the word lost its meaning, Jakindra dreamed of Clementine, every memory her mind could muster and some her heart conjured from wishes. She woke to her tears floating past the wide uncovered windows.

They sparkled like stars transported within arm's reach.

Forth, the Wicked, Lovely Lie — 5,781

The ship had 2,627 official names at last count —at least one for very planet it visited and more from each one's cultures. A number of the inhabited moons and stations it passed had written it into their legends, warnings and religions, using whatever appellation best spoke to that population. In English, when Jak boards, it's called Forth.

It had been The Dearly Departing but the name struck some too morose, a macabre joke that conjured up the war that had transformed the ship. Forth was now unrecognizable from the ship that had launched decades before, utterly foreign in social composition if not material structure.

War on a ship did that. No one knew of another ship that had survived it and if anyone would know it'd be the inhabitants of Forth.

Such confined violence stripped things to their atoms. You saw exactly what they were made of, people and parts. No reinforcements would save you; you could not escape. You and those who surrounded you became the universe even if the real thing waited just outside the hull.

Walking under the soft lighting of one of the ship's vegetated, serpentine hallways, Jak could not have guessed such a past. Back on Earth, Clem used to say Jak was no good at guessing. She must have been right because she hadn't guessed Clem would be back on Earth and Jak here on the ship they used to watch together from the dusty, desert floor. She sighed.

The ship's past was one of the first things she'd been told when she arrived. The rest would come with orientation, Janas, the human who showed her to her quarters told her. An older White man, Janas hadn't said much in the way of welcome, only the time and place of her orientation meeting and just before he walked away, with his gaze distant and voice wistful, "this place is a wicked, lovely lie." He'd paused, fixed his gaze on her, "Hometowns always are."

Then he'd left her, unsettled, with her thoughts.

"Left, please," the guide in her earpiece said. "You are here."

Jak stopped in front of a bright white archway. It was lit from within. The flowering vines and ivy did not grow on or within a foot of the archway. They wrapped themselves around a thin underlying structure that stretched from where the floor met the wall, up to the ceiling and back down to the opposite junction. Leaves obscured whatever anchored it all. From that point forward the walls, ceiling and floor were white, except for a thick green band of color down the middle of the floor that stretched from just in front of her into the room beyond the archway. She followed the stripe of color. In three steps she found herself inside an immense room with sunken seat rows, each row lower than the previous one, all of them encircling a central space at the bottom level.

"Welcome to the amphitheater," someone said.

Two folks, a human and an Uyep emerged from either side of the back of the room. They stood, as she did, on the top level.

"I am Carac," the man said.

"And I am Ufrazengi Mondesh," the flemg said. "We will facilitate your orientation."

They walked down to the bottom of the amphitheater, stopped at opposite sides of it.

"Please join us," Ufrazengi Mondesh said.

Jak began to descend the stairs, straight down the middle.

"You may stop if you're uncomfortable," Carac said.

She paused for a second and glanced at him, then took the last steps until she stood between the two of them, each one a few steps away. She'd never seen an Uyep in real life, not flemg, flemp, flemt or flemz. This one was only four or five inches taller than her and just taller than Carac. The flemg's face was wide, flat and fleshy. If pressed she'd call the skin color golden though Ufrazengi Mondesh's limbs, both arms and legs as well as the extenders that protruded from each shoulder and fanned out into a scintillating plume of skin and scale, were yellow in places and bronzy black in others.

Carac sat; Ufrazengi Mondesh hovered.

"Please, take a seat if you like," Carac said.

She did. Carac continued.

"We find it's best if visitors and residents of Forth learn our history from the very beginning to help them decide if they are a visitor or a resident.

There are two options for orientation: a neural implant, which can be used for syncing and communicative purposes should you decide to stay on Forth or the neighboring quadrants, or an immersion unit. Are you familiar with these technologies?"

Jak shook her head.

"I've heard of them, but they don't really exist where I come from. They do on the planet, just not where I'm from."

"A neural implant is a device—"

"I understand what they are, just not how they work," she said.

"And you'd like to?" Ufrazengi Mondesh said, interest turning up the volume of 'like'.

"I understand your concern," Carac said. "There's no need to be afraid; both are very safe."

"I just want to know how they work," Jak said.

"The neural implant is a combination of Earth and Mtzlit technologies. It is inserted just above—" Ufrazengi Mondesh began.

"I don't think that's what—" Carac interjected.

"No," Jak said. "That's what I want to know."

The Uyep made a sound of appreciation, somewhere between a hum and a whistle, clearly one of interest and assent. The flemg continued in ever greater detail, while Carac crossed his legs, ankle over knee and watched, bemused.

After a few minutes Ufrazengi Mondesh finished and held Jak's gaze, smiling, humming.

"Which would you like, Jak?"

Her name sounded different though those lips. There was a definite pause after the 'k' as if a silent syllable had been added at the end. Though not quite sure why, she liked it.

"No implants. I'd like the portable immersion unit," she answered.

"You're aware of the potential synchronicity issues? Should you chose to wear it while performing other activities, you'll co-experience." Ufrazengi Mondesh said.

"I understand."

"Shrewd choice, Jak." Ufrazengi Mondesh responded, a smile in the flemg's tone.

Jak returned the smile, stretched her legs out, feet cocked the flemg's direction.

"Exceptional," Unfrazengi Mondesh said, looking over at Carac. They shared a look.

"When would you like to begin?" Carac asked.

"Can I start now?"

"Yes, you can."

*

The fitting went quickly; in less than an hour Jak's earpiece had been repurposed to house the immersion unit. She had control of the full complement of its fields: visual, auditory, tactile, neural, and blocking tech. She could go as far in or not as she liked with a few taps of her left finger pads on one other, her thumb and palm.

The sessions could play out in the background of her thoughts as she moved throughout her day on the ship. The neural implant would have wired her to a system. Having been born free of such links Jak aimed to keep it that way. It would take something powerful important to make her change her mind. The neural implant also concentrated orientation into five continuous time units. With the immersion, she could spread them out, leaving time for long looks into the heart of creation.

Ufrazengi Mondesh and Carac suggested a phased approach for her first time, and that she dedicate her consciousness to the experience, alone, without any outside activity. So she returned to her quarters and turned the blocking tech all the way up, chose 'Phased' at the prompt. With a tap of her pointer to her thumb she dropped in.

The Wicked

Jak saw black. A woman's disembodied voice, the same one she'd chosen for the earpiece, spoke.

"Welcome. In this level of immersive orientation, first person accounts of The Break are available. You may choose to immerse yourself in one of the survivor's experiences or enter as yourself. Please choose from these options."

Text materialized in the darkness, the letters a dim, glowing silver tinged in blue.

Arah *Each person was allotted 5 kilos of cargo. They said they had room for us, but people brought the dumbest shit with them—all the bad habits and poison judgments of the dying world. Tons of them. We knew that the ship would buckle under that weight. It's a wonder it didn't fall out of the sky. When it gave way it pinched us poor first.*

Bevel Hah Hayden Szhat Sibor. *There were days I couldn't believe what I'd seen, days I couldn't believe what I'd done. I watched on vid once as a black hole pulled what must have* *been a level's worth of bodies into its belly from half a galaxy away. Like they were being called home or to heaven or hell. I can see it now, just talking about it. You don't forget such sights.*

Kinjal *You couldn't hear anything. All the yelling and screaming. Even that, it just became like, nothing. There was so much that it stopped being a noise. It was just like, life— this is what it is when you're awake. Folks used hand weapons, for fear of breaching the hull. Do you know the sound it makes when metal splits bones? A horrible wet thunk. It cuts through every other sound. That's how horrible it is. That every other thing just fades away, slinks away, goes away. You hear* that.

Andy *We cleaned for a year. The corridors were filled with blood and fuel, things I couldn't identify. You can't air out a starship. You can't sanitize people's memories so now we have this I suppose.*

She chose herself.

The text faded away and the black blinked out to a cavernous room with bunks lining the walls, folks running, alarms blaring. Jak sat on a lower bunk, near the middle. Sweat stuck her clothes to her skin; she found it harder to breathe. The black blinked back on, but the noises, heat, and small weight of anxiety on her chest remained. The blinking continued. The room. The dark. The room. Jak realized the lights in the room were flashing.

"Shit. They finally kicked it off," someone whispered on her right.

She looked over and saw a man there, outlined in the dim. His voice, the shape of his hair in the dark made her think it was a White man.

"No time for sleeping, love. Time to be on our way," he said as pulled something from under his pillow. The lights blinked on. It was a pipe, nearly as thick as his freckled forearm.

"They were right to," he continued. "If the ups keep rationing the oxygen we won't be able to fight back. Now's the time." He pulled a jacket on over beige sleeping shirt and pants. She looked down; she wore them too. On second glance, they all did. "Have you no weapon?" he asked.

She looked around the bunk, felt under the pillow and mattress, bumped into something hard wrapped in plastic. She pulled it out, unwrapped it. A flashlight heavy and cylindrical. The thing looked like an antique. She clicked it on. But it worked.

"Clever," he smiled at her and stood. "I'll follow you." She looked at him, bewildered.

"Follow me? Where?" Jak asked.

"Above," he said dipping his head up. "Where else?" She considered giving him the flashlight, looked down the long row of bunks until she saw exit symbols over a far door. Jak bent over, flattening herself against the thin mattress and felt the floor below. There, boots. She stopped to put them on.

"Hurry," he said, breathless. "They're cutting it. Can't you feel it?"

She could. The room swam when she stood up. A group ran in front of her as she made her way to the door.

"Julian!" She turned, saw two more men join the one following her, Julian apparently.

"Where's Batu? And Keisha?" Julian asked.

"Haven't seen them. Probably already above."

None of them paid her mind, but neither did they stop following her. The lights went out, this time for good: even the exit symbols extinguished. She blinded an AQ in front them without meaning to. All its pupils shrank down to pinpoints. Jak swept the beam away, illuminated the group of folks lined up behind it, each with their hands on the one in front's hips, shoulders, appendages, whatever limbs they could reach and still move. She could see why. This dark was absolute. Wherever they were, no light reached. AQs could still see of course; they always could. Jak hoped she remembered the exit's location.

The AQ gurgled: "Yes, this way."

Jak looked at the AQ. Odd. That had only ever happened with her best friend, Clem; the two bore no resemblance.

"Clem is not of our number then?," the AQ said to Jak. The wet in its words made it hard to decipher. "Let her luck continue."

"Don't you know to shield your thoughts?" Julian said to Jak.

"It's not the one to worry about," one of Julian's friends said.

"There will be others," the AQ added, "on the restricted decks." It turned to Jak. "Think of colors, the lyrics of songs. Try to remember a smell. These things can shield you."

The door swung open and a column of light beamed out from it. A figure stood in the doorway.

"Keisha!" Julian yelled.

The figure at the door nodded her head in acknowledgement, looked their direction. As she took a step back to let folks out, Jak could see her more clearly. Her clothing differed from theirs. Its dark material fit her form. The shirt sleeves ended just below her shoulders, exposing chiseled arms only half concealed by dreadlocks swinging past her collarbone. A red braid ran down the length of her pant legs. It looked like a security uniform.

"Come, come, come, come!" Keisha waved them forward, her hand circling her wrist. She looked away from them, up at something in the hallway. Air rushed in from the corridor; that as much as anything spurred Jak along. When she finally stepped through the threshold she could take a deep breath.

A horde of security with batons aloft descended on them. Jak turned her torch's beam into their eyes as the others set in with pipes, bare hands and teeth. Even the children. Shock turned to horror as one of the security guards reared back with his baton and knocked a little girl sideways with a blow to the head. Keisha dodged a tackle and kicked that guard in the ribs, once, twice, felling him. Then Julian finished him with a blow as Keisha moved on, up toward the front of the group, taking the lead beside the AQ. Jak fell in just behind them.

Their group pushed through the corridor as a column. In the first hundred feet, they learned to gather at each intersection and turn as one. On the third such turn, an odd clank sounded from further down the corridor. When they reached an open door where the sound was loudest Jak looked inside.

Long chains hung from the ceiling. As the chains swayed they came into contact with metal stirrups attached to a trio of gurneys hovering over anchor docs. Soiled and bloodied bedding hung from the gurneys, brushing the floor. Jak squinted at the stirrups. It took a second to recognize they had shackles.

From then on she kept her gaze forward. When she didn't, little horrors visited her from the periphery: galleys where vermin stuck out of pots, some butchered and some feeding; emaciated children, mourning the moment or their mothers, Jak couldn't be sure.

Folks in the back invited them to the middle of their group; a few joined.

They reached a large, round room with descending rows of seats and high ceilings. Jak recognized the amphitheater if not its current state.

Folks filled the space from the sunken center to the back wall: AQ, humans, Tillers, Uyep, The Still, Creshian, Adamanian, Sotoh and Itue. She didn't recognize the rest. They gathered in groups, talking, gesturing, standing silently and touching, using all the communication Jak could catch and some she couldn't. She recognized the weapons easily enough. A Tiller towered over the others, handing them out.

This is their staging ground, Jak realized. Their forces gathered here.

Jak meant to stay in the amphitheater and take it all in, but Keisha came calling for her light, then squinted at her when Jak held it out for her to take. She didn't just want the light.

Jak followed for a step until the woman took her shoulder, and firmly, gently, brought her up to her side.

"I can't protect you back there," Keisha said. "And you can't show me the way."

A light in the dark indeed.

It took a crush of guards with stunners and gas to separate them. In a great push into the ups' main reception level Jak guessed wrong. She took a step away at the wrong time and couldn't reach Keisha's outstretched hand before a great gate crashed down, leaving Keisha inside and Jak tumbling back with Julian. One step and they would have made it. Now

Jak and Julian along with dozens of others were penned in. The ones who entered the ups' haven scattered as gas began to fill that space too.

No one entered the space where Jak and the others were trapped, coughing. They didn't need to. With walls and gates on every side they posed no threat. Still no exhaust clicked on to clear the gas. The humans, Uyep, Tillers, and the Still hacked until they passed out or finally cleared their breathing passages. The others watched, waited, lent what comfort they could.

Jak's light lasted a long time. When it blinked out she crouched down. It felt safer somehow. She listened to Julian devising plans above her and later to his curses when those plans failed. Jak wondered where the AQ was, remembered its advice and thought instead of creosote back on Earth, the way it smelled of rain in the desert. At some point her head fell forward and she jerked awake.

Breath, all she could hear, and heat all she could feel as the oxygen fled. She didn't need Julian to tell her. The struggle in her lungs sufficed. As her eyes adjusted, the outlines of the people around her emerged.

She closed her eyes; struggled to open them again, felt consciousness slipping away as she snatched a bit of air into her lungs. She edged past panic into something worse.

"You have reached the end of the recommended time allotment for your initial experience."

Hyperventilating, Jak fell sideways out of her chair. She hit the floor with a jab of pain in her shoulder. Her eyes snapped open. She saw one hand trembling out in front of her. She stared at it as she wrestled her breathing under control, watched her hand still, felt a tear streak across her temple and soak into her hairline.

Slowly she unclenched, then flopped onto her back. Coolness reached through the fabric of her shirt and pants. She stretched her palms against the floor, spread herself as flat as she could, so that all she felt was that temperature. *That's all you can feel. That's all you can feel* she told herself.

It might have been the first time she lied to herself, in all her days.

*

On the next go, Jak took a different approach. She turned the settings down, chose to immerse herself in a survivor's experience, and ran the simulation in tandem with her first solo explorations of the ship and the basics of life on it.

She donned clear-framed, round-lensed looking glasses Carac supplied and tapped the right temple, launching the experience she'd chosen. The woman's voice instructed from the temple's tip.

"For best alignment it's suggested you begin in the main garden, the same physical location as the lived experience."

Jak tapped the left temple, pausing the playback. The main garden. She thought back to the layout of the ship she'd worked to memorize. She could call the information up with the earpiece, but she intended to learn the ship sooner than later. Jak turned left and found an elevator bank, decided on the fifth level before she saw the locations listed next to the buttons in the elevator. She called the elevator with a push. Seconds later, the doors opened to two Uyep and one of the Glen conversing softly in a language she didn't understand. They nodded as she entered. She returned the acknowledgment and looked over at the buttons, pressed the one with '5' in its long line of symbols. She'd chosen correctly.

As the doors opened on the fifth floor, light flooded in. Jak stepped out into it. From the wave of pleasure that washed across her skin she guessed the light must be UV. She stripped off her light jacket and, finding an empty bench a few feet away, laid it down next to her as she sat.

Whereas the ship's vegetated hallways contained vining plants and ivies the garden housed flowers and hedges, fruiting trees and climbing ones, succulents and rainforest flowers lined up in neat sections, each one its own mini habitat. She gaped at the variety. How many worlds' vegetation was she looking at? She decided to return here and explore, but first a different discovery.

Jak removed the glasses and rubbed her eyes, took a closer look at the subtle circuitry visible in the clear frame and put them back on. She'd already cued up the playback. Jak pushed the glasses up at the bridge, and with a tap at the temple she dropped in.

Her perspective shifted to a bench catacorner from where she sat in the garden, the one under the star-blossomed tree. She felt constricted. Looking down she saw delicate fabric stretched over a stomach billowing out before her, and on top of it two pale hands, human, pasty enough that the thin blue veins of his hands stood out clearly. The fabric didn't give. He shifted and pulled the front shirt tail clear of his pants, resettled. His pointer finger vibrated; he tapped it to his thumb. A voice, respectful but urgent entered his ear.

"Sir, we highly recommend that you return to your quarters."

He exhaled brusquely, harrumphed his dissatisfaction.

"I do not entertain your recommendations, Sergeant. I will have my peace."

"Sir, there are now disturbances on all eight sublevels. Communication at both the sanctuary and lido district has ceased. This has all the markings of —"

"Is it not your responsibility to serve and protect our caste?"

"Yes—"

"Then go do it. I'll not be ordered about by a man who is employed at my leisure, who breathes oxygen at my leisure. I am Lionel Betrand."

"Yessir, I only mean—"

"*I wasn't finished!* I am Lionel Bertrand, heir to the family who launched this ship, descendent of those who picked the rest of you up from your godawful holes in the galaxy and allowed you to remain upon this vessel gainfully employed and ensconced in our hospitality and *I will be treated as such*! Is that clear?"

"Yes—"

The discharge of a small arm laser singed the wispy blond hair on the back of Lionel Bertrand's left hand. Snapping his head to the left he saw a group of workers, human and alien, firing from in front of the main entrance. Two, now three of the Aerie caste fell. Their handhelds and jewelry skittered across the garden's brick walkways.

To his right, the entrance to the restricted passageway back to the Aerie beckoned. He looked around at the others of his caste—at least four other lead families, but none closer than him. Fools; he'd chosen his bench purposefully.

Lionel dropped to the ground and crawled forward as those around him fell. A shot heated the space next to his head. He crawled faster, hazarded a look back. The shooter's attention moved to a family running toward the exit and Lionel took his opportunity, standing and bolting the last few steps.

He slammed the door shut behind him and held onto the handle, braced his slippered foot against the wall and leaned his full weight back as those on the other side yelled and struggled to open the door. He gritted his teeth and strained. The sound on the other side grew more frantic, from yells to screams, then cut off. Jak felt a wave of disgust as finally the door settled in its frame and the force that had opposed him ceased.

He let go of the handle and turned.

Three men, clad in mechanics coveralls stared at him from the entrance to the passageway to the luxury quarters, and the Aerie beyond them.

He yelped as the closer two lunged at him. Lionel ran into the closest tunnel, slapping through a shallow stream that ran down the middle of the curved floor. He heard "Stop!" as he came to an intersecting tunnel and ran into it. The smell of human waste entered his nostrils and mouth, nearly overwhelming him. The three didn't follow. He gagged, pressed the crook of his elbow over his nose and mouth, as he leaned into the wall. Which way? The smell worsened in the direction he was headed. Blinking to clear his head he searched for an exit, an entrance, any respite. A low opening near the bottom of the tunnel stood halfway between him and where he'd entered this section. He dared not go towards the men, but wasn't sure there was another way. He hunched forward. His eyes began to burn. He closed them, took another step and sicked on himself.

The force of it pushed him down to one knee, closer to the stream and smell. Again the vomit came, and again. Shuddering he prayed his stomach had emptied. He looked at the low opening warily and made his slow, pained way there.

Taking a cautious step out to see around the corner he spied the tip of a workmen's boot and jumped back. His head sunk low as he got down on his knees and then his belly, the offal soaking into his clothes and covering his skin as he looked through the opening and, seeing a dim light beyond it, jammed himself through inch by eternal inch.

Jak thanked the immersion unit's designer for including sensory control buttons and Carac for suggesting she turn them down.

Lionel had no such options. When he finally tumbled out of the opening and smacked into metal grating that covered the entirety of a dim, dank room, Jak realized they were in the waste treatment facility that manufactured the garden's fertilizer. She appreciated the closed system if not the specifics that composed it. No doubt, Lionel had never entered it or its environs before. No wonder the men didn't follow or wear respirators. They probably worked in this area of the ship and knew it wouldn't be his reprieve.

After a few seconds waiting and listening for footsteps, Lionel got up from the floor and stood. Behind a centrifugal pump and check valve—his exact thought was 'bundle of things' Jak noted—two manual doors stood.

Lionel hurried to them and opened the one closest, heard yelling and quickly shut it. He opened the second and leaned into its blackness straining to hear. Jak knew he didn't see the ladder that led from the bottom of the door down into a tunnel or the catwalk that was retracted into the other side of open space. He hadn't looked down or out. She braced herself. Lionel stepped into the nothingness and crashed down.

In a heap at the foot of the ladder he cursed and wiped at the tears—sweat, he told himself—falling into his open mouth.

Still, to Jak's irritation, his unwavering, undeserved luck held as he looked around and noticed the huge ventilation duct that lined the far wall. In other parts of the ship, she knew people were running out of oxygen and couldn't find passage, but this orchestrator of inequality, one of the leaders who'd lay this long fuse had stumbled onto what might be the easiest and safest way to move now. With a phillips or a small-headed driller he could go where he wanted. As she watched him, she realized Lionel didn't know that.

Scared of making any noise and not recognizing the releases that surrounded him or even the recessed tool boxes built into the head of this duct section he felt around the duct, trying to detect a seam where he might pull it apart.

Given this ship was built some time in the last century, he was unable to find one. Jak's vexation grew. With no choice but to settle in, she watched as he took literal hours to locate the embedded segment release on the underside, never mind the activation sensor or two other manual releases, and climb into the ducting. The reward for her patience was another tumble into the dark when he lost his grip and crashed through an atmo vent affixed to a ceiling. This time Lionel lay unconscious.

Jak paused the immersion. She opened her eyes on the gorgeous garden. A warm light fell across her lap. A blue blossom floated past, but she only felt anger. It seethed and bubbled as she tried to find a place for it in herself and the lovely landscape that surrounded her. Two humans and a ~Shlin~ in coveralls walked past her bench, nodding a hello. She nodded back. This helped. The present was better, better than a rich man with a poor intellect who couldn't find his way into a quick release tunnel.

Jak steadied herself with a breath, fast forwarded a bit and dropped back in.

She sat, flinching every few seconds, in a security tower perched on a promenade that overlooked the main thoroughfare. Flinching because chair after chair smacked into windows that wrapped the promenade. They bounced off, but each one left a thick, ugly mark. She feared that soon there'd be cracks. Or rather he feared. Jak watched as whirl of emotion she couldn't separate filled her. She felt his fear, but also her own fascination. It unnerved her.

The two of them took a half step forward, looked out and down to the open floor below where chaos collected.

Folks covered the floor, crumpled and cowed, fatigued, and fallen, dotting the space like stepping stones. Freedom fighters tripped over them as they pushed forward and helped the fallen up or out of the way. Then together they beat at the barricades pressed against the outer doors as well as the ones that led to the security tower.

Three groups entered the space below, each from a different walkway. From their clothes, Jak guessed them to be security, freedom fighters, and the old ship's wealthy upper caste, or the ups, as Julian called them.

They clashed in the middle; then something peculiar happened.

The groups began to break apart. Two of the security personnel attacked the upper caste group and another went after the freedom fighters. One of the freedom fighters pushed another off an up he'd pinned to the ground with a boot to the neck. The up was turning bright red, each vein in his forehead visible even from the tower.

"Not him!" the fighter, a Black man, yelled. The security guard yelled something Jak couldn't understand and lunged at him. Then she heard clearly,

"All of them!"

"That's Finneas' son. The one who stopped the rationing!"

"McGee? He sent the rapists down!" another fighter yelled. Together they took on the security guard, wrestled him to the ground.

From all the groups, half a dozen of the others fell back completely. They didn't run or attack. Just eyed each other warily as their weapons and hands slowly drifted down to their sides.

More folks entered, went after each other and the groups already fighting. Two of those who just entered, a human woman and Uyep flemt, battled ups for a few seconds on the floor and then kicked their attackers away and scooted back toward the walls with the other observers, sending them scattering until the flemt and human that joined them held their hands and extenders up. It became a universal sign as surges of folks filled the room and ended up in one space or another.

Blood, hair, fur, flesh, scraps of clothing collected in the middle, was beat into a mushy layer of filth whose streaks, from where they stood, showed the passage of lives, from this world to the next, and of time.

It went on for hours.

The more Jak and Lionel looked, the chaos coalesced, showing an order that did not bode well for him, but there might be hope depending on what he chose when the barricades came down,

The observers let the fighters punch themselves out, even kill one another, but not come after the rest. When they tried, fists and batons beat back the intrusion and settled again. Once a threat was neutralized the observer-protectors backed away until there was no space left to retreat. By default a circle formed around the fighters who would have it no other way.

They kept going until the only ones left standing, stood together. Jak wouldn't have believed it if she didn't see it herself.

Jak watched as folks broke through the barricades and came for Lionel. Even this close she didn't know what he would choose. He seemed pragmatic enough to lie if that's what it would be, but arrogant enough not to.

In the end, he did not disappoint or particularly surprise her. But then, she didn't actually know him and he hadn't earned her faith. Jak supposed it didn't really work that way, which explained some things.

*

"You did well, Jak," Ufrazengi Mondesh said.
"What does that mean?" she asked.

"You chose to end the immersions before they overwhelmed you. You also didn't take the opportunity to inflict pain on others when you could have."

"All a test then?" Jak said.

"Not all. What was, you excelled in. You never even feared me. We need to know who you are—as much as *you* do anyway and as much as we can through these methods."

Jak chose her words carefully.

When she finished she felt certain the Uyep had a clear understanding why they were called curse words.

The Lovely

Lovely is the life that leads you home begins the inscription on the outside of Forth's funereal ports. Four chutes in the starboard side composed the ship's facilities for last rites. After a night of uncanny dreams, filled with flashes of Clem's face and the soft strength of her shoulder pressed against Jak's exactly as it always felt when they walked through sandstorms and sunsets alike, Jak sat across from those words, atop a small bench she believed placed just for such reflection.

Ufrazengi Mondesh found her there.

"Are you still angry with me, Jak?"

Jak didn't reply. After a moment, her gaze turned to the floor in front of the flemg and then up until their gazes met.

"Would you like to try a different immersion?" Unfrazengi Mondesh asked. "I can promise you a very different experience. I think you may enjoy this one, and for the right reasons."

"But do *I* think I would enjoy it?" Jak asked. "That's what matters."

"It's what came after what you experienced and the resultant tribunal. How we came to our current state, the first anticolonization missions."

Jak looked up, caught the flemg's gaze.

"Anti—" Jak began.

"Anticolonization missions."

"On Earth, we were told you were a commercial vessel."

"That is not surprising. In some cultures there is no word for what we do or what we are as a group— and in others, no acceptance. To acknowledge it would give it shape and weight in worlds that would deny such possibilities, to some or all. But it is real. We have done this. Would you like to experience it? It is an essential stage of our development."

"Yes," Jak said quickly, "I'd like to see that."

*

Jak chose to drop in from her quarters. She dimmed the lights, checked that her mattress was flush with the wall and spread her blanket out on the floor alongside it. Satisfied she'd have a soft place to land, she slipped off her boots, looked up to confirm the locked light on her door was illuminated and reclined on her small mattress, tucking her earpiece and new blackening goggles into place. With a deep breath, she began.

Green titles materialized in the darkness.

Cree *a new home*   **Qezzel** *returned lands*

Yebantaq-3 *a dissolution*   **Ead-Urk** *gives its world*
of the colonies   *away*

She wanted to experience them all. After a few seconds of deliberation Jak chose Qezzel, closed her eyes, activated the experience and opened them.

"It looks like Earth," a young woman, human, brown-skinned and black-haired, said. Her hair was cut short, nearly to the skin. Jak could see a tattoo of geometric patterns on her scalp. She stood near Jak, where the observation deck came to one of six points, backlit by the planet's beauty.

Jak had to agree. This planet had far more land masses, or upon closer look, one extremely large landmass and a few others a quarter or less of its size, but on the whole, it did remind her of the receding Earth that frequented her dreams: the background of blue water, the white swirl of atmosphere and clouds, the bit of green surrounded by gold and brown.

"Cresh," a Creshian said, catching the woman's eye. "Cresh as well."

A ghost image of a planet, almost Earth's negative with green water surrounding small islands of blue flashed in the center of the room. Cresh? Jak wondered. Then she sensed a whisper of sound at a frequency higher than she could truly hear. She only knew something had happened by the quiet that followed. Jak looked around the room, caught sight of the group of ~Shlin~ huddled together on the wall; they'd boosted each other's signal to communicate the image.

The planet reminded them of ~In~.

Would they resettle on the planet below? Who would receive this jewel? Jak studied those on the observation deck. She'd not met some of these kinds of folks before. A shimmer of light at her elbow stole her attention.

"Excuse me," she heard. Jak's eyes widened as the shimmer solidified a bit. She couldn't discern a body shape but she couldn't mistake the smile that greeted her. Jak nodded.

"No trouble at all," Jak said, watched the being fade as it crossed the observation deck. How many more had she missed, and for how many reasons? She shook her head slightly, surveyed the room, peering into its dim corners and taking stock of what she could see clearly. Eventually she looked back out at the planet as it grew closer, larger, and its characteristics came into greater focus.

An announcement echoed throughout the deck. Jak couldn't understand the series of clicks, tones, and words. She felt the excitement building in the room, looked at those around her, trying to suss a clue. Folks started to file toward the exits. Jak walked that direction. Halfway there, the English translation began.

"Please join us at Airlock 6. Those who wish to observe the repatriation may disembark through there. Upon your return, medical clearance will proceed from Airlock 11. Teleportation is disallowed for the Dearly Departing. Only the prodigal Qezellen are permitted on the teledeck today. Thank you for your understanding."

Jak joined the queue. It was long, long enough that she missed the final descent, only felt the ship make contact with the ground. Once through the airlock, she was not handed a helmet like some others. Nor did she seem to require the thin blue jumpsuit some stepped into. She waited. For the moment she couldn't see anything but the folks in front of her.

Finally, they exited onto a field. She couldn't quite place the purple vegetation that covered the land from the ship's site to the impossibly tall mountains that encircled the valley where they'd landed. Jak looked closer trying to categorize it. It rippled and pieces broke free or lifted into the air though Jak felt no wind.

"My god, the butterflies," the black-haired woman said.

Butterflies. Jak felt a twinge in her chest. Her breath caught. *This* is what they looked like in real life. Real life. She blinked, tried to regain her bearings.

As she did, clusters of lilac Qezellen materialized in the valley. Already they were legion, and growing. Bipedal, the shortest were as tall as a tall human man. A few were easily twice that height. She presumed their legs were the same as humans, but their arms had extra joints. As they looked around, their arms undulated in waves of motion from the shoulders out. They stared in all directions, toward the mountains, one another, the flowers at their feet, the butterflies in their wind, the sky where still more of their number moved invisibly from the ship to the ground.

Many Qezellen wore bright red, great billowing blouses that moved in the windless day. Jak wondered at their lungs or whatever part of them that kept the fabric filled. The pants, skirts, shorts differed in shape and cut, but they all wore that style of shirt, and they all wore all red. Jak took these as celebration clothes.

New groups arrived one after the other, filling free spaces that had a second ago contained only butterflies and blue sky. Jak felt excitement build along the line of folks from the ship who watched. They shared small looks with each other, tiny touches on

49

shoulders and backs as the scene before them unfolded.

She had never seen so many in an open space. Nor had she ever seen so many cry. A few Qezellen doubled over or crumbled to the ground, holding one another, an apparent family group, themselves.

One of the Qezellen, male she thought, ran past her, switched direction and tore off up the valley straight through the folks filling it. To those who faced him, he reached out his waving arms and they waved toward him. Where they made contact a puff of mist formed until he left a trail that followed him into the center of the group. There he stopped and leapt into the air. When he landed, he jumped again, on a beat the others seem to know. The people closest to him joined in, their rhythm built onto his beat but didn't match it, and out the leaping, rhythmic circle grew, touching off at the edges and in between.

Then the singing began. In that they matched one another, sounding off at the same time, at just the right time to close the loop and pull it tight enough to gather round them, their jubilation vibrant and huge, shaking the earth beneath them.

Jak felt it call to a small plot of emotion in her, eager to join and spread. She stood there laughing quietly, dancing a bit, long after her legs started to ache and she grew parched, until the ship had to leave. They all did.

Even as folks came to coax them back in and they reluctantly allowed themselves to be pulled that direction, they looked back, trying to remain with it, this unyielding joy.

Laying in her bed, moments after she surfaced from the immersion, Jak held onto the unit after she'd removed the clip from her ear and goggles from her eyes. She stay there in the midst of the memory for hours. She couldn't shake it, didn't want to. It had been her best company since Clem.

The next day she found Ufrazengi Mondesh. She had to know more about their anticolonization missions.

"How? How do you do this?"Jak asked.

"There were many ways: returning lands to those they were stolen from, or to ship-born slaves who never had them, finding dead worlds and revitalizing them for symbiotic union."

Her mind stuck on one word.

"'Were'? You don't now?" Jak asked.

"We've learned we cannot."

"'Cannot'? Why?"

"Because we need this ship to survive. Not just for our survival. For the survival of those we encounter and can still help. We amassed a tremendous knowledge in those decades spent finding, reclaiming, and providing homes. What we've learned we may still teach others. We cannot make peace by starting war."

"Starting war?" Jak asked. Anger tinged her tone.

"Many saw the missions as acts of war. Even on uninhabited or abandoned planets, if only because they sought to exploit the resource at some supposed later date. This is not a war vessel, Jak.

Our shields are outmatched by more than half those we might encounter in this quadrant. Only a quadrant of a galaxy, and we are vulnerable. We do not help those we seek to if they are dispossessed or enslaved once we leave or intervene. Every action is an opportunity—for good or bad. So now we who remain on this ship seek to increase the probability for good by sharing what we have and what we have learned."

Jak furrowed her brow and pursed her lips, looking away.

"Your time here is an opportunity to find your home, an opportunity some never have."

Ufrazengi Mondesh emitted a high hum Jak hadn't yet heard. Even from an Uyep she recognized the tone of disapproval. She looked back as the flemg continued.

"Some live on the ship; some choose an earthen world and leave this place forever; others may choose a different kind of life on another ship, station, or moon. I know a sect that chose a comet. Some come back here, but all who are medically cleared have the right to come and go. We've found that space requires such freedom, and more, that the soul demands it.

We've also come to agree that each of us has a soul, a shren, an umm, at least one. We choose the name that suits us. The universe is full of useful words. You and I converse in English because it's easiest for you and I've adjusted my translator enough that now I can approximate all I mean to say using these words."

Jak knew that Ufrazengi Mondesh meant well, that the flemg explained to soothe her anger as much as share their truth. And though it didn't square to Jak, she couldn't see how it ever could, she exhaled and tried to accept at least some of what the flemg offered.

"Your language has more words?" Jak said wearily.

"Our language has less use for words. It has less words, but they suit me better."

Jak considered that.

"One must find what suits," Ufrazengi Mondesh said. "Your language has some effective words. It articulates what it is we do here, now."

"And what is that?"

"Sankofic development."

"Sankofic, like sankofa? 'Go back and fetch it'?" Jak said.

"Yes."

"One of those words isn't really English, it didn't originate in it," Jak said.

It was the flemg's turn to contemplate.

"Each requires the other," Ufrazengi Mondesh, responded with a smile and the humming noise Jak had come to think of as a smile, mostly because Ufrazengi Mondesh had taught her to by doing them at the same time Jak realized.

"Sankofic development dictates our routes, of the individual and the collective. One cannot exist without the other—certainly not in this environment and possibly in all of them."

"Sounds kind of random."

"It is the opposite. Forth is a life, a way of living. All ships are, all planets and stations. We here, you and I, are in the enviable position of choosing which way."

The Lie

Jak stared as the ship crossed through Oteko's upper stratosphere and slowed, dropping gracefully as a spider on a string. Ice covered Oteko. Tulo the capital of its northern region sat atop a crag, an ochre-colored crystalline structure that hovered, impossibly wide, like a spinning top perched on its tip. Ufrazengi Mondesh had asked her to meet for tea and drak. She leaned against the railing that lined the band of windows. A small clear shelf with a cup holder and depression pulsed out of the railing near her hand. She placed her plate of drak on top of it, her tea in its holder, and watched as the depression molded around it. She crouched down and peered at the bottom of the shelf, searching for sensors. Perhaps that small slit on the floor or that bump near the railing. It could be the railing itself. There was much to learn. As she stood, Ufrazengi Mondesh approached, humming a welcome.

"Another test?" Jak asked, her tone even.

"Oh . . . no. A homecoming for Janas. I thought you might wish to say goodbye. He was the first man you met when you arrived on the ship."

Janas hurried past. She didn't know the old man could move like that. He flashed a smile their way.

"Goodbye," he said. In this light he fairly beamed; though Jak hardly knew him she couldn't help but return his grin.

Janas waved and hurried on. Jak settled in next to the Uyep and looked out the window.

A moment later the telltale displacement of air in the shape of a wide beam marked Janas's transport from the ship to the surface.

"Forth always goes back, you know," Ufrazengi Mondesh said.

"What do you mean?"

"How many times did you see us in Earth's atmosphere before you decided to make your escape? We don't intervene, but we offer. It often takes more than one, especially if the inhabitants have lost the ability to recognize it or haven't yet developed it. And then they must find a way.

Or consider Otero. We were here when Janas was a boy. He first saw snow on this planet, first met so many who looked so much like him. He's talked about it ever since. If his parents had allowed it he might have never left Otero the first time. But in that period we only took the parents' opinions into consideration. I am glad for him. I doubt Otero will be what he remembers, but hope that what he wanted remains what he wants. The past can be a lie."

"He said something like that to me when I arrived," Jak said. "That this ship is a lie."

"It is," Ufrazengi Mondesh agreed.

Jak grew quiet.

"The lie is that we're a ship. It may have been in the beginning, but even then it cruised the galaxy picking up peoples like souvenirs and turning them into servants, then refugees.

Forth is an escape, a traveling classroom, a library. A choice for those who choose differently. It has been other before; it will be again."

"Riddles aren't wisdom," Jak said quietly.

Ufrazengi Mondesh made an appreciative noise, tapped an order into the small pad that pulsed out from the railing.

"Have you heard the one about possibility?" Ufrazengi Mondesh asked.

"The riddle, the lie or the joke?"

"That there are limits. You tell me which it is."

"I used to tease someone the way you tease me," Jak said.

"I only wish to tease something out, Jak." There it was again, that endearing, punctuating silence at the end of her name.

"Did you like this person you teased?" Ufrazengi Mondesh asked.

Jak smirked.

"Your primary acclimatization sessions are complete," Ufrazengi Mondesh said.

Primary. Jak grunted, watched the swirling snow dance across Tulo's architecture.

Ufrazengi Mondesh asked, "What have you learned?"

Jak looked the flemg in the eyes, then remembered the Uyep didn't like direct eye contact or weakness and adjusted her gaze a hair higher, making sure not to make it seem a mistake.

"I've learned if you're lucky," Jak said. "there's a lie that's holding you back," she paused, looked at Ufrazengi Mondesh for a second. "If you're not, there are many."

"Well spoken," Ufrazengi Mondesh answered, meeting Jak's gaze and nodding.

She wondered how often they all adjusted for one another, and if the others thought about it anymore. She looked forward to when she wouldn't.

"What did *you* learn" Jak asked. "In your orientation?"

"So you *did* like this person, the one you teased." Ufrazengi Mondesh said and leaned back a notch, humming.

"I learned —," Ufrazengi Mondesh waited for Jak's full attention as her gaze drifted back from the snow, "you don't have to convince others in order to save the world."

"Which one?" she asked.

"All of them."

*

56

Is that what they were doing? Jak wondered after Ufrazengi Mondesh departed. She stood on the observation deck watching Janas' new home grow smaller, but no less glorious. As the planet receded, Jak blinked back surprising moisture in the corner of her eye.

She couldn't say why exactly. Her thoughts collided. She'd seen more in the last few weeks than in a life already filled with heartache and triumph enough for a woman five times her age: nights in the desert, mornings in the graveyard, miles walked without mother or friend, weapon or whistle should something come charging from the dark. Jak had found and lost Clem, forgotten her father's face, launched into space. She'd been abandoned, sold by strangers, and exchanged her fear for something handier, a dexterity that freed her before they ever touched her face, broke her will, smothered her special.

And in all that she'd never felt pinned to a place. Not even one as lovely as Qezzel or another with a true friend. Would it leave her wanting she wondered, this never having a home, the lack of longing for it?

It's not what she'd been seeking when she and Clem blasted off. She only believed herself bound for something better, even if that better only lasted a few minutes.

But Forth felt like a calling, though it didn't speak her name. It had a heat though, the fuel that drove it, that righteous reordering and creation that progress required.

H748-K—

Undetermined

Jak, is it how we imagined it? Do the stars seem close enough to touch? Do you eat every day? Have you seen a meteor yet? Tell me everything.

We're not at the Gog anymore. That's why I have access to a console. One day, about eight months ago, it rained so hard the whole western side of the tenement fell in and took half of the rest with it. Bo and her boys didn't make it. Some other folks died too. It took two days to dig Grand out. I've never been so happy to see anyone. She was covered in muck and blood, holding the last of the vegetables to her chest like they were part of her. I decided before she could say anything that we had to leave, and that day we did.

We made it to Texas. It's not too different here but it's higher ground and they still have watering holes in this part, not all high grass and sand. That's better. Plus the chance to send word to you. Grand's been exploring at night, searching for clay. I've been turning oil drums into kilns for the woman who owns this console. It's not a challenge, but I get this reward. Write as soon as you can.

Clem

*

Clem!! Everything I see I want to tell you about. I do actually, in my head, but great shit, I miss you. It's not the same. So good you're some place better and that Grand is good. Terrible about Bo and the boys though. No one left to hang the white banner and no where to put it. I said words for them last night.

I wish I could explain how it is here, but you're better with words than me. So I'm sending images. See that first one. That's where you are, and what it looks like from out here.

I wish I got a picture of Earth when I was closer, but I forgot until it was this far away. It looks so smooth and clean, right? Those perfect edges and deep colors. You'd never know how rough it is once you're on it.

The next one is where I am. Those are my quarters—3 meters square, quiet and clean. A table flips down from that wall. So not quite the shiny whoa we thought it might be but I like it. There's no dust here, not anywhere on the ship. A static field pulls the dirt, loose hair and the like all straight down to trash receptacles that hold it for terraforming donations. You can feel the stir of it at your ankles sometimes, but that's all the wind there is.

I thought you'd like that pale one with the cracks and white. That's Ganymede, one of Jupiter's moons. Jupiter is all that blurry coral and white color behind it.

Tell me more about where you are and how you are. It's been too long.

Jak

*

I never thought I'd see you use an exclamation mark; two is incredible. Almost as incredible as those images. Gorgeous, Jak. It's just gorgeous where you are. Soak it all up for me.

I miss you too. I can't believe it takes so long for your messages to reach me. Seems like we've waited long enough.

I'm making the most of the time between.

I've started on a new project. They have a scrubber here. I told you it wasn't much better, but at least they can clean their air. The scrubber's half-broken, mostly because no one maintained it—either didn't know how or didn't think it had to be done as often as it does. I gave it a once over and now they want me on a bigger fix. An H748-K, total rebuild. Dream shit, Jak, if you dream of hard work. And I do. You know that. That's the kind that comes true. I can see you smirk at me, but it's true. It's also a great distraction.

There are a lot of fights here. Mostly with outside folks who don't want to follow the rules at The Exchange. The Ex is like it was back home, but on a bigger scale, big enough that they could get shit done if they put their minds to it. It's not just a few folks bartering for necessities. Everyone has something to offer here; if you think you don't, some sweetenough might take pity on you, but everyone else might just watch you starve to teach that lesson to newcomers and kids. It's effective. A man tried and came back the next month skinny and ready to trade. It's the doing that works here, not the having. Even if you own it it's because you built it yourself; otherwise you could be labeled a thief. I'm fucked to know what they do if something's left to you when your someone passes. People don't die as often here.

See that schematic I sent you? That'll explain it better than I can. The design trumps words. Just your thing.

Their system is a great start, but it could be improved. They could buy and sell terraformers if they cleared all the deadwood projects and put people in the right places, doing the things they already know how to do. I'd try to convince them but they don't listen. So I'll just work on getting this H748-K up and let them see for themselves. It's not really a terraformer, but it's something we could use onplanet. Terraforming Texas should be proof enough.

Then we'll see what we can build from scratch. Remember that pirate radio we made to listen to those old hem haws squabble and the staticky orbiting DJ? It only cost time, determination and spare parts. They've got more parts here than they know what to do with. I mean that word for word. It's not as much as the Gog (I brought the best pieces I could carry), but the pieces are new. They gleam without being rubbed with sand and spit. They have barrels of oil here. It would be so easy; things should slide into place.

Let me know where in the sky to look for you. On which star should I wish?

Clem

*

No one builds from scratch here, Clem. They don't know how, but they have knowledge. There's a library here I couldn't have even imagined. It makes anything we had on Earth seem tiny. More even than the universe, I wish you could see this library. It is a universe. No one here has ever read it all and I doubt anyone could, well maybe the Sevael but that's because they almost live forever. I learned that at the library. I'm learning my trade there too.

It's massive—takes up a huge room, a quadrant of the ship really, but mostly it's accessible through a bank we have access to, like a console but a lot smaller and no buttons or anything just these black cubes you lay your hands on and manipulate to navigate around a projection. You would love it. Everyone has access to it, but not everything—not the things you could use to kill someone or a planet, to control any race of beings. That's the way it's always said, with foreboding. It took three sleep cycles to stop thinking about that.

On the ship, we choose our own days—how long they last. It helps find what you have in common with other folks, the ones who chose the same kind of day as you or just whoever's awake at the same time. And when I say folks I mean everyone, The Central, The Glen, Uyeps, humans, Shraps, Womazu. Everyone is folks. It took a minute to get used to that but now I quite like it. In the beginning, learning it all, some days I was tired not long after waking up. So sometimes I'd just stare out the windows, take meals in my room, or think of you.

I'd love to be next to you trying to raise that H748-K from disrepair. You like that word? I do; I learned it when I got here. It just means left to shit, but sounds nicer. Sounds like something you'd say. Like something I'd tease you about.

What'd you think of what I sent you? Remember it? I still had that sketch of Beast in my pocket when we left. All the things I wished I'd said that day Clem. I know it wouldn't have been enough.

Thank you for finding me out here. Anything I can do, you let me know, Clementine. I'll do it.

Jak

*

Jak, you're doing it. Just be you. And you're listening to me. That counts.

No one listens here. They won't learn how. I keep telling them that the filters need to be changed out and replaced with polymer ones, that the hydropower motors can be broken down and made to drive the scrubbers but they won't listen. They'd rather watch seal after seal crack and blow a motor I just fixed. They don't care when the lights blink out, or more folks start coughing, or someone steals a scoot in the middle of the night to brave the desert on the way back to the first city where the O_2 booths still work.

They didn't even listen when I told them about the thieves! The tool thieves here will take anything that's not pinned under you when you sleep. So that's that I've started to do. I've slept better, Jak. At least at the tenement you only had to worry about flash floods, sandstorms and starving. That's a joke, Jak. Har, har.

They've stolen two torque wrenches, the bender I spent three months making, and the calibrator that got us though last winter. Was that only last winter? It's unbelievable you've been back in Arkansas that long.

Grand found one of the wrenches and tried to convince me I'd given it to her all along. It just chafes me that they'd bring her into it. I wish they'd stop, but machines can only fix so much. They can't right these people's conniving ways.

Remember those beaches Grand showed us images of? Will you land? If you do try to get an image of a beach for me. I'm sure they still exist somewhere. I keep dreaming of them, sometimes right in the middle of a screaming hot day, on the walk back to Grand's I dream I'm at a beach and this is all a vacation, and just beyond the dunes there's water, oceans of it, clear skies and a warm, soft bed beyond the choking haze. I've walked towards it once or twice. It can seem so real, Jak. It's . . . impressive.

So's the H748-K. I brought it back and went beyond. I'm working on something custom, making it better with the parts on hand. I haven't figured out its name yet. I will though, I just need to get a moment away from work to rest and think clearly. When I'm not on the job, the rest of the day is a daze. But working on that 48-K is balm, better than any I've used for the sunburn, wracks, or other the maladies that plague this place. I can't believe no one had been keeping it up, or a dozen other things they could do to better manage life here.

The problem with the people here, including the thieves is they're afraid.

Fear makes them mean, but it doesn't solve a single problem. So I don't try to scare them with the inevitable outcome of all this inaction, but it's scary shit, Jak.

They had a meeting and called on folks with concerns. I tried to convince them it wasn't frightening, but to fix things they'll need to do what they never have: believe and let that belief inspire them not to follow but to lead. But I can't count on them coming to their senses. I have to take care of myself and Grand, play my part.

Here's what I've come up with for the 48-K. I'm working on a new draft, but wanted to send this schematic now. This is my ship, Jak. It may not take me from one planet to another, but it'll move us into a new world, one where we can finally put these masks down and really see each other again.

Clem

*

Clem,
Are you good? I've been trying to think how to say that so you'll hear me, but that's the simplest way. You said so much in your last message and some of it I

couldn't follow to be honest. Are you sleeping? Getting your minimums? Has something happened you don't want to tell me about? You can. You can tell me anything.

I'm not in Arkansas. I hope you know that. You're writing to me on an IS console; you don't need that to contact people on the same planet. And I've been gone 7 years. There was no winter for me last winter.

When do you think these thieves started stealing from you? Is Grand around? Would you ask her to write me? Please, one of you, write me back as soon as you can.

Jak

✧

Clem,
There must be some kind of news. I've enclosed a few pictures of Saturn's rings. Let me know what you think.

Your Friend, Jak

✧

Clem,
I hope you'll answer this message. Did I say something wrong? Are you just busy with the 48-K? Obsessing over those shitmagnets where you live? Did the

console go down? Whatever it is, just send word. All this quiet is creeping.

Love, Jak

✧

Jak stepped into her quarters. She walked to her console and called up news from Earth, selected North American, then scanned through the Texas entries. Nothing.

She added Clem's and Grand's names to the search and turned on audio playback, increased the volume as she walked toward the corner, pulling her boots off. She tossed the right one into the corner, let the left one drop from her hand as she turned.

"Pause," she said louder than she meant to. She took three quick steps to the console. "Rewind, repeat," she said softly.

The report started again, but Jak hardly registered it. She heard a woman say "I wouldn't say I know her. We traded; everyone trades here. Her grandmother died in some kind of disaster and she ended up here," but then lost the thread of the report.

Only the accompanying image broke through Jak's haze: Clem, covered in dust with someone's blood covering one side of her body. It wasn't hers, Jak could tell, if only because of the dead-eyed stare on Clem's face.

She knew it was Clem though the image blurred her facial features. She could tell from her height, even the way Clem stood next to the man she'd murdered.

But for her expression, it could have been Clem on the 20th birthday they didn't celebrate together but planned. Just as Jak'd imagined it would, Clem's body had grown lean and strong. If not for that machete in her hand and the distant smile up at the security drone it could have been her on that day, down to the way one hip was cocked back, ready to walk through the next obstacle.

Afterworld — 31,282

The ship hung in space, shimmering, commanding, massive, as if it spun the blackness that surrounded it as a suitable backdrop for its beauty. Afterworld had presence that spoke more of stature than simple existence. As if the sparks of light that rippled across its hull showed the darkness' depths in a way nothing else could. As if the molded Creshian ore that covered it had seeped up from the surface of that planet's cracked mantle so it could one day cover such a creation.

Ela, head of the Denark Group and sole director of its planetary holdings, a brin never impressed, was.

She reclined, eye stalks quivering, in the back of a chauffered shuttle, taking it in. Another of today's sycophantic voice messages vibrated her handheld. She knew that's what it was. They all were. She tapped the thing silent, shifted in her seat, enjoying the silence, the view and the textured, massaging fabric beneath her.

The ship must have been four times the size of any craft Ela had seen. The star cruiser that carried her to Centauri Alpha See, the now-former standard bearer of massive vessels, didn't compare.

Afterworld was a Class 3 Paradise ship, not officially World class, but it had the girth, the shape and much of the grandeur, though a subtler, more confident version she surmised. Father would have been impressed if he'd seen it before she sent him there.

Though rumored to be financed by a shadowy group of ex-monks bent on targeted reincarnation, Afterworld came highly recommended by the most prominent families and corporations in the system. And it only took comatose patients. It couldn't have been more perfect. Ela unfurled her feet from their folds and relaxed.

A victory unsavored hardly qualified. She inhaled, let the air bubble through her, draw her back to calming thoughts, the mantra that anchored her.

Confuse, convince or circumvent.

Father told her the paths to success when she was just a nymph and taught them the first time he'd said "no" to her and she found a way to get hers. She'd had her sweets that day and would have them again today. She'd outgrown candied arthropods but seeing him this last time would yield a satisfying crunch.

She empathized with Father's love of power. He craved it in a way she understood. It's why she'd bought him this last luxury even as she reveled in the spoils of his century heading the council that allocated funding, food and Donalani laborers for each hurrah.

Ela bought him a forever he would appreciate, a heaven that could satisfy that craving more completely than wealth, family or even power ever could. She knew what that would mean to him, but not what that meant for him, so she brought him here to the people who would find out and the place that could generate it.

His lesson served her well, even enabling this moment. When she couldn't convince him to hand over leadership she, with the proper mix of coagulants and time, circumvented him. Even if he couldn't appreciate the efficacy of his tutelage, it deserved reward. What better consolation than his own personal heaven?

Judging from the view, true to form, she'd chosen well.

The shuttle slowed as it reached the docking section on the far side of Afterworld. The pilot didn't warn her about the bump when they entered the ship and landed, or even get out to open her door. Odd, but taking a closer look he was only part Adamanian (and probably Donalani Adamanian at that), the other part human or Shrap. She couldn't tell them apart and anyone who said they could had too much time and too little understanding of how to use it.

A wonder he'd passed the flying exams. She made a mental note to request a company pilot for the trip to collect Father's body when the time came. Though she had to make the trip to save face and keep leverage, she saw no reason to compromise any further.

A second before she reprimanded him Ela heard the seal hiss as the pilot disengaged it and, from his seat, pushed a button to open the door. She collected herself and slid out and down the airstairs, pleased to see at least the staff here knew how to receive a woman of her eminence. Three of them stood shuttleside ready to greet her.

Elam Ritan Ela, welcome, the Adamanian signed to her.

"We may communicate verbally," Ela replied. The Adamanian nodded curtly, taking the correction in stride. No need to feign intimacy because they shared an ancestry. Let them all speak one language and conclude their business quickly.

The airstairs creaked behind her as the pilot descended the steps and walked away. When she glanced that direction he was gone. At least he had the good sense not to hover over their conversation.

"My father?" Ela said.

"This way, Elam," said another of the attendants in a thick brogue Ela couldn't place. Where did they find these pritzak? No matter; ultimately the appearance of care mattered more than the actual level he might receive here. Already tongues wagged over how she'd spared no expense for the Chancellor's final days.

This too would bring her quarry.

*

Stijn lengthened his stride as he exited the docking area and entered a small vestibule that separated it from the rest of the ship. He had 17 minutes before he would be expected to check in or depart. That was the pilot average Mercure gave him. He had to reach Engineering 1 quickly. He'd only obtained the schematic this morning and only the corner that abutted the docking area. That 30 minutes of feigning ignorance was worth it, though it almost got him pulled from the assignment he'd worked four months to line up.

Afterworld widely advertised its client list, but he knew military sites with more accessible infrastructure.

He reached the door, opened it. The corridor was empty. One bit of luck: the massive ship had less than 3,000 crew so he should be able to move freely without encountering many of them. Surveillance would detect him of course but shuttle pilots had authorization for this section of the ship. The blue strip of lights running along the floor matched his badge, confirming that.

He turned a corner. Doors lined this walkway. Only those of unoccupied lavatories stood open, revealing the bright overhead lights reflecting off the wash basins but not the further facilities the schematic showed behind bulkheads. He stepped into a lavatory. The door slid shut. Here he could escape the cameras though his heat signature would be recorded and retained for 24 hours, standard protocol in the system. By then he'd be back at Mercure HQ, debriefing the others.

Stijn lowered himself onto the middle commode seat, ignoring the hole and vacuum hoses altogether. From his jacket, he retrieved the small case he'd brought with him. Only 3 mickles wide, it resembled a smaller version of the toiletry bag human pilots carried; its contents differed.

He pulled a bir board out of it. No thicker than a playing card it easily slid behind the door's electronic lock. His hand lingered there as he let the bir board's coding do its work. A soft vibration buzzed across his hand. He pulled the board out and tapped the corner. It had accessed the circuitry back as far as the engineering terminal. Far enough for him. He tapped again, pulled up the schematic for each primary section.

A small projection of the ship's schematics hovered in front of his face. Dense with detail, he had to enlarge it just to see a fraction of the conduits, the ducting, and circuitry, steel, densofal, and whatever else kept this leviathan aloft. He chose a section and enlarged, again and again, spun the schematic right, then down, enlarged, zoomed in, twice more. Stijn marveled for a moment at its intricacy. At the edge of convolution, the design broke through to something breathtaking. Pity, he thought briefly. But that die had been cast. He couldn't bring his mother back, nor the 80,000 other Donalani workers she'd led and died with and he wouldn't waiver now. He inched the schematic with his fingernail, just left. That spot would start it going in the right direction. He slowly moved the schematic further to the left, and there. Down and zoomed. And there.

That should do it. He didn't need the last charge, but Stijn believed in contingencies. He synced the locations with his nav and flushed the commode. Stijn splashed two bracing palmfuls of water onto his face before he put the bir board away, pushed it past the detonator and charges in his bag, and opened the door back onto the corridor.

*

Clem had given her permission to watch. It was the last thing she said before she went under, the first lucid word Jak'd heard from her in too many years.

Really it'd been a request; Clem said she didn't want to be alone in the dark.

So Jak spent her free time monitoring Clem's cog cycles, as she prepared to do now. Jak stood on her side of the clear partition that separated the ERCR chamber from the observation lab. Enhanced reality cognitive redevelopment didn't require a team once the cycle scenarios were initiated and stabilized. So she stood alone. As donor patients entered new states of their redevelopment, adjustments were made, new scenarios created and revised, but Clem wasn't at that stage yet and the other members of her group were stable at their current stage.

Ideally Jak would have explained the cycles to her long-lost Clem before she went under. There'd been a lot she'd wanted to say and hear from Clem before then, but when Jak finally got Clem released to Afterworld's pilot program her old friend was catatonic. Not just Clem but dozens of the people brought from Earth to Afterworld for treatment. Their malady had a name now: Sudden Stress-Induced Psychosis Syndrome. Doctors couldn't call it Brief Psychotic Disorder anymore. It was no longer brief; nor was it still rare. That whole generation, Jak's generation, were susceptible to SSIPS. After she'd left Earth (the only reason she'd left Clem), SSIPS emerged and invaded. The number of cases nearly matched the prevalence of pulmonary disease.

Now Jak did what she hadn't, she stood by her. Jak'd lingered on Afterworld long after its test phase. As its designer, she'd done her due and more, but the crew seemed to welcome her extended stay and she couldn't think of any other place in the universe her time was better spent.

Others in the industry begged to differ. She scanned through two more offers as she stood there reading the message on her handheld. At least they had the sense to message first. The more industrious sorts showed up at Afterworld knowing things they shouldn't know, or explaining how their project could enable her to apply established tech to new applications as she'd done here with quantum computing and nextgen VR applied to cognitive redevelopment.

It sounded good if you didn't listen too closely, but Jak had a weakness for details. Her specialization in difficult cases took her to worlds on the verge of transformation. Their beginnings and ends yielded incomparable insight to those willing to look. Details enabled her success and recognizing bullshit, her peace.

She closed the messages. Nothing new there. She glanced at the door, thought of the CP's office. Perhaps there'd be time for a visit after this. Best to use the quantum computer while she still had access to one. She'd not found a better distraction than tasking the tech with equitable projections of future states and the best way to attain them given current resources and probable transient conditions. She spent hours asking the chief programmer, Tadda, how to present information to the QC and learning the best practices to get the information she wanted. Invigoratingly fascinating stuff. She'd spent months on projections, huddled away, the chief programmer the closest thing she had to a friend.

The only force that could have distracted her from that lay on the other side of the partition, inside a capsule whose circuitry Jak had once dreamed up for exactly this purpose: to do right by the one who had unlocked the possibilities inside Jak, the ones that she now brought to being.

Before Clem, Jak was a tumbleweed, pushed by forces beyond her control. She hoped to do something similar for her friend. Jak hadn't anticipated entering Clem's cog cycles to do that, but the sandstorms and flashfloods of their youth taught Jak about anticipation's shortcomings, and the years since, traveling this galaxy, learning her craft reinforced the value of being present to create a future.

Jak looked through the partition that separated the observation room from the ER chamber. A full bank of 15 capsules lined up neatly in three rows of five. All were long-term participants. Each had their own optimum conditions inside the capsule: temperature, air mixture, light, cushioning or lack thereof, angle, pressure, music and humidity. Clem in her capsule, eyes closed, breath even, lay in the middle row nearest the partition. She looked peaceful in the heather gray shift all the participants wore. Jak put her earpiece in; its tiny mic extended just beyond her ear lobe. She twisted the mic gently, removing it and placed it in her pocket.

"Hey, Clem," she said softly. "I'm coming in."

Jak took a seat at the cog console that stretched across the room's back wall, cued up #6's controls, entered her security code and patient authorization. Her right pointer finger hovered over 'Initiate Entry.' She wondered what would be today's tale.

Clem's cog cycles were stories she told to herself. Others had no such layers or ontological distance the doctors and techs said. Clem was special they told her.

They didn't need to.

Jak inhaled, initiated. Clem's voice had deepened and grown gravelly since their days in the desert, but still it soothed her. It slowed her breathing, even here and now in circumstances young Jak and Clem would never have dreamed, that they would now only meet in dreams.

***   ***

"Blue was a golden city nestled in the foothills of a mountain range with a forgotten name. Forgotten only by the city's inhabitants because nature held so little value in their lives. It had been defeated by the vids, the technocratic spoils of civilization, but mostly by the commercial wormhole that sat high atop the peak of Mt. Zo, whose name they knew only by association. Only the few who took the bullet train to work there learned the full name of Mt. Mizotashon: they read its deep print as they passed the entrance gate.

On a not-too-distant crag stood the only other building that overlooked Blue. Seen only from a distance, they called it the Cube. Inside it at 4 am one humid summer evening Clementine stood. She stared at the blue flame of a newly lit match bursting into life. For that split second it illuminated her face in the semi-darkness and her shale brown eyes drank in the light. Jak watched her from the pedestrian bridge above the portal.

Through the floor to ceiling windows that made up the eastern and western walls, a diffused silver light from the wormhole spread through the room. —"

***   ***

The wormhole world again. Clem spent most of her time there, arcing out to far-flung bastions of the observable universe and beyond. The doctors had their theories about this, that over time Clem would travel to ever-closer destinations until she rejoined with the storytelling part of herself, the part of her that knew that the ERCR wasn't real, the part they hoped would one day wake from the cognitive cycles and move on to work therapy amongst the crew, that caught Jak's eye even in catatonia whenever Jak came close. The doctors thought she was working through grief over the past.

Jak understood that it wasn't regret. Clem just knew how to make the most of broken parts, always had. So now she lived the other life; the one she hadn't chosen, and Jak was part of it. It made her hope that she'd come back, if not to her than to this world.

A voice interrupted Jak's thoughts.

"Crew, your attention please. You must evacuate. *Now*. This ship. Will. Soon. Detonate. Make your way to the evacuation shuttles . . . Do not dally. Do not doubt . . . Save yourselves. Any attempt to remove patients will trigger a detonation in the oxygen stores, annihilating the ship and all chance of survival."

*

Running his finger down the projection, Stijn checked to make sure all channels carried the broadcast. Annnnd, yes, even the subpsych so any doctors that might be writing realities shouldn't be caught unaware.

No need to check the corridors now. Anyone he might encounter should be running for their lives and wouldn't pay attention to one more person doing the same. Stijn crossed the room.

"Het is een eer, moeder." He activated the countdown, left the door behind him ajar.

The way he'd come was blocked with folks: humans, Adamanians, The Central locomoting along the walls. He couldn't see them but suspected there must be Sotoh and Itue as well.

He'd synced three routes to get him back to the shuttle. The pilot ruse was still his best way to remain undetected. Chaos worked in his favor now, but on the other side they'd perform checks. He needed to beat the first wave and miss those if possible.

With a last look to make sure no one followed, he turned left and took the stairs up. He'd cross over and back down to the docking area.

*

Jak jumped to her feet, ended the ERCR link.

If she could find it, she could stop it. She took the mic out of her pocket, jammed it back in her earpiece, switched the channel.

"Engineering, call up surveillance for the last 12 hours."

"Right away, Architect," came the response. Trusty Oldean.

"Oldean, security has been mobilized?"

"Security has fled, Architect."

"What?!"

"The permanent detail was detained for medical clearance. Those onboard are contractors and this facility offers no insurance or death benefits, Architect. This quadrant—"

"You're serious?"

"I am."

Jak emptied her lungs, stared up at the ceiling trying to think.

"Oldean, evacuate."

"I will not, Architect. The ERCR guests are capable of—"

"I'm sure they don't know about the ERCR guests. They're not part of the marketing. *Fuck*! I told them to lay off bragging about the big names." Jak walked over to the cog console, began the sequence to transport all ERCR folks to safety. "Oldean, the ERCR guests, evacuate them."

After a long silence, Oldean responded.

"Yes, Architect."

"First please start a full trace and intruder recon search, all channels, all access."

"Already begun."

"Send the results to me."

"Done."

"Go, Oldean . . . I've prepped Room 174. Start the other release sequences." Jak looked down at the console's countdown. *8 minutes 13 seconds*. Please let that be enough time.

Jak looked at the capsule that held Clem. She'd need 90 seconds before she could be moved at all. Then the chute under her capsule would open with the others, sending them into their evac cars. They'd link up to the VS drive shuttle and set off for the nearest full service station. Jak couldn't take the time to say or do anything more, needed to, tore herself away and ran out the door.

Her head collided with someone's chest. She took a step back, and pivoted to continue on her way. She glanced up and knew immediately who she'd run into.

He wore a pilot's uniform, but wasn't one. Or at least that wasn't all he was.

Pilots didn't rush to pick up detonators rolling across the floor.

Hell of a time for no security. But really she never had any. She pivoted after all.

"You're making a mistake," Jak said to his back. He stopped. She had one hand on her weapon, concealed under her shirt, but didn't yet intend to use it. Faster to learn the location than search for it.

"You see these rooms?" Jak said. "They're full of folks who—"

"Folks who've wiped their asses with others," he said, voice full of venom.

Jak stopped, blinked. Considered.

"Not these folks," she waited a second. He didn't immediately attack her or shout her down.

"They're survivors. And now you want to kill them. For something they didn't do. They survived world wars, famine. Some of them their whole world poisoned. Asteroid showers that killed continents." Jak could feel her anger swelling.

"They come *here* after. After the world tries to kill them! But just ends up destroying their minds, their spirits. And we try to bring them back. These folks?! They didn't do whatever it is that's got you blowing up ships. Not them."

He turned to her, his expression tight, eyebrows knitted together. Those protruding eyes, those hands. He was Adamanian, at least part.

"Who are you?" he asked.

"No one. Just someone who wants you to know what you're really about to do here."

"Answer the question."

"I'm Jak. I designed this place."

"You?" he asked. She heard the doubt in this voice.

"Me." She let the edge poke through when she said it. This time she let the anger steady her as she continued. She spoke quickly, not knowing how much time they had.

"This ship is built around a karmic mechanism."

He squinted as he listened. Jak continued.

"These rooms hold survivors trying to rebuild their internal worlds by working in a virtual one during cognitive cycles. Those cycles, their byproducts and the energy they create contribute to the energy that sustains the paying patients, the comatose privileged. The ones I assume you're after."

"Then get them out," he said.

"We could, if you give us time . . . but maybe you'll give us more." Jak clasped her hands together, pushed her words out in a rush.

"15:1 that's the ratio that sustains this place. For every chancellor or warlord, 15 survivors have some place to heal . . . and they don't owe it to those rotholes. The rotholes can't survive without *them*. That's the design. One fucker needs 15 people to have his heaven."

She turned her palms to him and spread her arms out, brought her hands up to waist level, looking him in the eye.

"I'm not making this up," Jak said.

He grunted, wouldn't commit to more.

"Let me show you. Is there time? Just one." She lifted her right hand toward the door behind him.

He took a step back, then another, stopped, stood and waved her forward with the slinky seven fingers of his right hand.

She raised her palm up to the reader, felt the fine prick of the DNA lock. Her design called for these in every primary section, Engineering included. They'd balked at the cost; so she battled and won them for this wing. If she survived this, they'd revisit the issue.

As the door to the observation lab slid open she tried to lose herself in thought. It had helped her find answers before.

Jak needed something strong and short. She didn't know anyone's cycles but Clem's yet couldn't tip him off that the chambers were emptying, lest he consider it a provocation.

Tadda once told her about a Sevaeli who had a single day that surpassed six centuries worth of heartache. Perhaps she could call up that sensograph. She doubted very much he'd allow the vulnerability of entering a cycle and even if she had a patient authorization she didn't think he deserved to enter any of their worlds, but—. He pushed her forward with one hand, his other on the detonator.

"I'm going to go to the console," she said.

He walked past her, reached it first.

"Access," he said.

She leaned over and input her code. He bumped her out of the way, his fingers already dancing across the v-keys. He shut down the security link and strong-locked the door.

Frustratingly adept. He glanced at her, then over his shoulder at the partition.

"Proceed," he said.

Chances are he was looking for somewhere to stick her or her body so he could continue on his mission with no more interruption. She needed to keep talking or execute other plans. She shifted her weight to the other foot, pushing the weapon tucked in her waist band closer to her right hand.

"Listen," Jak looked behind her. He stood at the partition, mouth slightly agape.

"You have Donalani fighters here."

The tone in his voice made her forget about the weapon.

"Yes," Jak said. "Freedom fighters fill this place. All kinds."

*

Ela waited on a chaise lounge in the alcove outside her father's room. She'd sent the attendants away. Who knew if they were involved in this little plot? Highly recommended indeed. Being Elam, she well knew that anywhere the wealthy congregated, even the comatose wealthy, perhaps especially the comatose wealthy she thought, was a target.

Denark Security had an ETA of six minutes. They assured her it would be sufficient time; they'd better hope. Ela tapped her middle fingers into the chair arms with such force that her fingertips hurt.

Five minutes, forty-five seconds.

And what to do with the old bresh? She stood and walked to the door of Father's room. How would it look if she left him? There was no time to pack him and his many tubes and machines along with her. No. Any fool could see that . . . She would cry, let her tears glisten in the camera lights and wage trade war on whomever posed the biggest threat to Denark's holdings, redouble the surveillance efforts (and be awarded the contracts to construct and maintain the expanded surveillance) and turn this in her favor.

She stepped away from the door, looked toward the exit.

Ela would tell them the truth: that she left her father in his heaven and his death was a detail over which she had no control.

He'd wired it cleverly. He must've brought options with him, consulted the engineering schematics and tailored it onsite. She'd locked those designs down, but not well enough. Regardless, she was dealing with a particular man, no two-bit anarchist. He understood precision.

Hopefully that meant she could understand him.

"You came in as a pilot, right?" Jak asked. "Then just go back as one. The crew learns from this lesson, and everyone onboard gets to stay in their world. Only some of them will ever rejoin ours. The ones you value. But they all have to be saved. That's the only way it will work."

Jak started to take a step forward, stopped herself as he raised his hand, the one holding the detonator.

"I'm not hostile to your cause," she said.

"Then give Chancellor Denark to me."

"If I let you leave with him they'll shut this place down for fear of it happening to the rest."

"This, what you've built here. It's not justice," he said.

"No, it's not," Jak agreed. "It's not even a solution. Technology never is. It's just a tool. Someone still has to use it properly. But this is what I can do."

He allowed a small nod, and for a second he locked gazes with her. She couldn't quite discern what she saw there. There were depths, but who knew where they went.

*

Stijn found her not far from where they parted, glaring through a window that looked out on the external docking station that shadowed the ship. Time to use the card not yet played. He used the full honorary, adding the obeisant term he'd practiced saying to remove the palpable disdain.

"Elam Ritan Ela Massafār," Stijn said. Her eye stalks snapped his direction, head followed an instant later. She puffed up perceptibly though issued no warning words.

"Permit me?" he said.

"Speak," she said impatiently.

"The shuttle awaits," he said.

"I've no need. Security will soon arrive."

"Security?" He dipped his head low before she could speak. "It is only this, Massafār. Are you certain they are kushkem?"

He bet his success on kushkem, "as they say," and its long history on Adaman. The same reason the Donalani were considered a different race though they had no genetic differences, the invention of hurrah hierarchies to justify their burdensome position in the culture, the concept that captured the natural order of oppression, the panacea for subjugation: Were they really as they say?

He could see her mind struggle to reconcile the facts with the doubt.

"Perhaps I could accompany you or they could accompany us back to a Denark holding?"

The irrationality of inequality embedded in their shared culture gave him purchase, and he took another step into her circle of familiarity.

"Perhaps I have misspoken and for that I apologize. My only thought is of your safety. As it is unerring, I bend to your will."

She brushed past him without a word, off in the direction of the airlock for the docking station. She passed within a meter of him, close enough for several of the micron trackers from the shuttle's textured seat to sync. He felt the buzz as it did, offered her a genuine smile as she departed.

*

The next ship day Jak welcomed the crew back, and was more than pleased to see the permanent security detail among them. She noticed Tadda admiring their form-fitting gear, smiled ruefully.

"We'll have to chart a new course around to the Donalani Field," the navigator, Esh, said, turning to Jak. Hir body moved like a wave from bottom to top until hir head swiveled into position. Esh made eye contact, hir red to Jak's brown.

"Why?"

"You didn't hear?," the navigator said. Jak raised her eyebrows, reconsidered if Esh would understand the gesture.

"About?" Jak offered.

"The Denark Group. Their rings are down. It appears the resistance finally breached their core."

"How?" Jak said.

But even as she asked she knew. A detonation at just the right velocity and location would destabilize that orbit, send every last bit of spy tech it didn't destroy out into space.

It wouldn't take much pop, more a matter of precision than power.

Continuum — 44

Jak started the sequence.

The next four minutes would dictate if she had spent the last 14 years, all her goodwill, and life savings wisely or fooled herself into chasing the improbable into oblivion.

As such, she took a moment for herself.

She walked across the gleaming black floor of the unpopulated main engine room, past the sequentiator, Engines 1, 2 and 7, the long glowing shaft of the central converter, and up five steps to the very top of the band of tall, wide windows that encircled this level of the ship. She'd included the view so that one could contemplate infinity just as much as see if, when the engine switched, the starboard antell blew itself and that quadrant of the vessel into the yawning vastness she expected Continuum to inhabit.

Jak'd aimed to design a spaceship with a wake. If it survived the next few minutes, Continuum would ripple through space, eventually changing design principles of starfaring vessels and, likely, planetary infrastructure.

She'd scoured Forth's libraries but found no record of what she envisioned; so she built it from scratch, incorporating the concepts and solutions that had pushed other ships into the upper echelons of achievement and efficiency to see if she could devise what might approach frictionless function and so run to the edges of forever.

In a perfect universe she would control who got the design. She owned it without restriction or lien but space was full of pirates, and one day someone would decode the quantum kernel that she'd never recorded, that spark of life that enabled the Continuum engines' (theoretically) safe transitions. But not yet.

For now the secret resided within Jak's mind, this ship and nowhere else. They were a singularity unexploded. She'd see how long that lasted.

Many engines comprised Continuum's evolutionary engine. They worked in concert, shifting from one to the next as each fuel source was exhausted. She took her cue from old internal combustion engines she and Clem had worked on as girls, then shifted her thinking so the goal became turning an engine into a kind of transmission, distributing power. She went a step further so that the engine also dictated which power it distributed. In Continuum's next phase she planned to base the entire system in componentization, making it capable of changing each engine's components as the need arose. Effectively this meant it could build other engines.

It was her fourth World Class ship, by far the smallest, but the first to expand beyond that form. More like a world than a world ship, Continuum was designed to sustain itself, and to do that, like a world, it had to adapt beyond its initial nature.

Her grandest theory hummed during its test. A slight charge traveled through the hull of the ship, sparking in the corner of the room. This was expected. The electricity dancing up from the waterfall crawled across its harness field and emerged in areas like this one for safekeeping and moments of delight.

That voluminous waterfall pouring through the middle of the ship provided the current power source. It crashed into deck 14 and pounded the hull there. One could hear it every time a door opened. Its calming effect had helped her recruit folks of the right temperament. Her wife, Tadda, said that between the tiny lightning and the condensation reservoirs on the lower deck she'd designed a ship with its own weather.

Weather was one thing; sustainability another. Only time would truly tell, but today would intimate its truth.

Jak crouched down and stretched out in a span of window between two vast black circuit banks, sliding her hand along the smooth facade of the polymer as she settled into the space and kicked her legs out in front of her. She crossed them at the ankle and relaxed her back along one of the banks. Her head fell back as she rested against it. The sole of her boot just touched the other bank. She'd measured the window seat specifically for this moment.

This is where she'd sit alone to see. The crew waited onplanet to find out if they'd have a new home for as long as they chose or guaranteed pay through the next fortnight and a cautionary tale. Only Tadda and one of the captains had insisted on staying with her; even that was denied. Tadda relented to Jak's gruff charms and as for the co-captain, neither one of them had a say about that. Jak had designed their contracts thusly.

Continuum was her ship. So in truth she was the captain; they just led the crew and made decisions informed by their expertise. Each first shift to a new engine was hers alone for as long as she might live. Which might now only be another three minutes.

She let her gaze wander out to the welcoming dark.

The golden perimeter of SubRet-28, half the size of Kax and twice that of Ead-Urk, shimmered in the gaseous purple cloud that surrounded the bright planet. Its sun lit it up from the right, far away enough that Continuum could dock here, but close enough to turn SubRet-28 into the beacon that Jak had followed here. From the other side of this galaxy she saw it and it seemed a sign of where to conduct the test. Never much for intuition, she still respected a feeling of uncalculated certainty.

Just 60 seconds now. She focused on the antell, drummed the fingers of her left hand over her right fist and tried her best to ignore the churning in her stomach.

Three distinct clicks from the sequentiator stole her attention. She glanced over. The converter hummed and its pale amber glow brightened to copper then green. Jak's hand trembled as she looked down to her lap and then back out at the antell. To distract herself she went back over the lists.

If it worked she would:
- Tell Clem
- Find a nonmilitaristic peacekeeping patrol worth donating a secured engine to, one whose work merited perpetuity
- Become a patrol in order to do that. Continuum would still explore, but they'd be on the lookout as well
- Thank Tadda. If not for the scenarios she'd helped her input into the quantum computer Jak wouldn't have taken this approach
- Expand the list of essential materials that might be used as fuel
- Create a starter kit of designs to share with folks of limited resources, thus expanding their resources
- Learn the finer points of perpetuity

If it didn't she had:
- Told Clem where to find her remaining designs and sent an advance payment for her work on them
- Shared a good life with Tadda
- Told Clem what she had meant and would always mean
- Seen more than she had ever dreamed
- Done what she had dreamed

Jak checked the time, closed her eyes.

She exhaled for the last four seconds, looked over at the shaft of the converter. The green glowed brighter, then, in long strands of silver, gave way to a darker mottle of color, and then to black.

To black.

She drew in a shuddering breath and wiped her cheek dry. Continuum was running on its next bank of energy.

Time to get going on that list.

The magnitude of her ambition revealed itself and Jak assented, activated her earpiece to call Tadda and the crew back home. It did feel that way she realized. While her mind leapt forward, a bit of her hung back and savored the feeling that accompanied home.

As she designed the details of her destiny, Continuum beamed her signal to the ones waiting, unsure of their role in the future she wanted to help shape, only certain that something would change.

Ours — *34-437*

Papahi found the book cover remnant in the rubble of the union hall that abutted her place. A crack ran down the length of the remnant; time had eaten away at the rest. Most of the pages had long ago powdered and yielded to the poisoned earth. Still, through her helmet's visor, she recognized it as a book, and that was treasure enough.

She couldn't guess the last time someone found a paper book on the South Island, in the rest of New Zealand or any other country for that matter. Pulping precious trees for words when none of them could fix things didn't figure, even if paper publishers hadn't all shut down.

She wiped dust from the readout on her oxygen tank and checked her levels. The air had a yellow tint, but hadn't yet formed a film on her exosuit. She had a few minutes before she had to get back inside. She gingerly wiped at the pages and they crumbled, returned to the dust from which they came.

They left behind, right there in her hand, more than anyone had the right to expect. It came in the form of a TIK speck, a nano bit of a chip enough to reconstruct the whole. Her oxygen intake increased from excitement. Papahi pivoted the exosuit on its left heel and trundled her way back to her outer door.

She couldn't wait to show the others.

As soon as the decontaminant seal opened and she could stow her tank and get back in her chair, she'd send word.

She stepped inside, locked the outer door and walked the suit to the washroom a few steps away. She locked this door too, swinging her weight against the big lock's lever until it clicked into place, activating the decontamination process.

When the inner seal snapped open she was already laying down in the suit, flat on her back, against the floor. With her gloved right hand she pressed the tiny yellow button between the first two fingers of her left glove and waited for the exosuit's body panels to fully extend up and away from her. When they did, she pulled off the helmet, sat up and flattened her palms against the floor behind her, then pulled herself free of the exosuit and along the floor two slides until she reached the wall holds inside the inner room. Reaching her muscled arms up, she grabbed the holds and climbed to the top one, swung her body over and plopped down into the waiting wheelchair. Leaning over, she released the brake, slid her fingers along the wheels' hand rails as far back as was comfortable and yanked the wheels forward as she sat up, launching herself across the room and to her console.

Papahi brought up a link. It took her straight to the Concourse at the center of the site. Only two others online, but Izan and Ava were a good start. Papahi's avatar dropped into the system.

It announced itself on the Concourse while the real Papahi powered up her camera and connected it to the console. Then she arranged the TIK speck in a patch of empty table next to the console, and turned on an overhead lamp. Small and grimy, the speck gleamed to her. Turning the camera on it, she presented it proudly as she leaned down into the camera's angle.

"I found this today," she said excitedly.

Izan's voice came over the line first.

"Pap, we talked about this! Stop going out there! What if one of your hoses gets a leak or your readout is wrong? It's not worth it. Not for—"

"Is that a TIK speck?" Ava interjected. "Can you zoom in? Is that an offworld edition?"

"Yes! Is it?!" Papahi refocused the camera.

"It's still not—" Izan began.

"Izan, a moment." Ava said. "It *is* offworld. Let me look up that ID."

Papahi clasped her hands together as the seconds crept by.

"Holy shit. That's from Continuum," Ava said.

"What?" Papahi said.

"No fucking way," said Izan.

"It's from Continuum."

"It's not."

"You want to check my decoding?" Ava asked.

No one checked Ava's decoding. One might as well second guess a calculator or confirm water's wetness. She'd once told Papahi being the only Black woman in Antarctica made one triplecheck everything that mattered. The cold might have receded but the environment could still be harsh. Papahi was pretty sure she didn't literally mean the only one but didn't doubt the rest.

"Time to wake up Aito and Hiroto," Papahi said.

"Doing it now," Ava replied.

Aito's eyeball loomed too close to the camera lens, blurry and disquieting. As he yawned he moved the camera down to his mouth then back so that his entire face came into view.

"Moshi moshi," he croaked.

"Morning, Aito," Papahi said. "Where's your brother?"

"Jikei!" Aito yelled. The yell ended in a cough.

The camera's mic picked up Hiroto's Japanglish cursing. It ended in:

"Kutabare! What?"

"Houmon. Concourse call," Aito croaked.

They heard Hiroto slapping around at his console. A few seconds later a light clicked on in the dark and he came into view. He was standing in his underwear, scratching his hip as he blinked into the light.

Izan whistled.

"What are you training for over there, Hiroto? You're getting enough protein to sustain that?"

"I'm training to come over there and kick your ass," Hiroto countered.

Aito laughed, gave his brother a virtual clap.

"Keep training, cabrón."

Papahi knew this was part of their routine, and there was real affection that went beyond the UN suggested strategies to temper suicidal ideation or VR isolationism but today it was hard to take the delay. Today they had real hope.

"I found what we've been looking for," she said. "A way to bring us together."

Aito sat up, picked up the pair of glasses he and Hiroto shared since Hiroto stepped on his two years before their next allotted visit, and put the glasses on before his brother could.

"You say that every time you find something, Pap," Izan said.

"Isn't it always true?" she responded.

"Let's see what you've found this time, Papahi," Aito said.

She moved out of the frame.

"Can I have control of your camera?" Aito asked. She gave it over.

"It was out in the solar workers hall."

"I thought we agreed you wouldn't go there anymore." Aito looked up into his camera, then back down at his screen. Papahi continued.

"I won't now. I don't need to," she said. She heard Aito typing, the echo of his typing across all their connections, then a soft hum a moment later.

"This attribution is correct, Ava?" Aito asked.

"It is," she confirmed.

"Hai?" Hiroto said, then whistled low.

Papahi lost the connection. Everyone dropped off and for a second she couldn't breathe. *Don't panic, just give it a minute. It'll come right back up. Don't panic.* She looked around the room, gaze searching for her mother's bark cloth that always steadied her, found it draped across a small chest near the bathroom. She followed the shape of the pattern, one square to the next as she waited in the quiet, the quiet that expanded in moments like this.

Papahi lived alone, rare in the Old South Pacific. Most folks lived with generations of their families, but she was the last of her line. Their homeland drowned long ago so now this interior part of South Island made a ragged reincarnation of the Tonga she'd never known. Her mother made certain that her culture lived on.

She'd swaddled Papahi in the dignity of it. The songs sounded different and the colors of the ta'ovala had faded but the soul of it endured.

When every other connection dropped she kept it, so even now the isolation didn't pierce her. She was one of a diminishing number in that regard.

In the sealed homes and apartments of the world, people kept living what life was left. In that she was no exception. What was exceptional was her mobility: Papahi went outside when she wanted, for as long as she wanted. She owed that to the collection of oxygen tanks that filled the back storage hall of her dugout in Mackenzie, and the family that assembled it. Before she was born, her mother used to rub her belly and tell her stories of how their family had collected them back when they started working on this warren. Then she told her stories of the stories she'd told so Papahi would stand firm in what she could accomplish.

'Not gonna start letting outside forces rule us now,' her mother used to say. 'We had a king, but never a master.'

Papahi learned that Tonga had never been colonized before she learned exactly where it had been.

'It doesn't matter where it was; it matters where it is: in you and me,' she'd been told. Papahi's mother had a talent for knowing what didn't matter. She'd told the doctors when Papahi was born, looking down at the twist of limbs that should have been two straight, well-formed legs. 'Doesn't matter how she moves; it matters where she goes.'

Papahi smiled at the memory of her voice as much as the story. How she missed her.

Now she had the Concourse. The site that housed it had been around for ages, back when there were websites. The site, buildabetter.world touted itself the crowdsource solution for a broken world, an alternative to the VR abyss millions fell into. On it, people started the bamboo movement with its mission of trapping carbon to slow the climate's change and bring back degraded land with little to no maintenance. The site attracted enough people to attract more—people with access, skills, means, every kind of person who found something they could contribute, some reason to stay in the world.

With the rich resettled in their paradise vessels and terraformed moons anything that offered a life beyond daily survival resonated.

"—hi" Ava's voice crackled back across the line, smoothed out. "Papahi?"

Papahi reached out and adjusted the volume.

"I'm back." She heard Ava exhale and Izan curse.

Who knew how much longer the links would last? Once the wrong satellite fell out of working order or the sky, they couldn't be sure when or if they could reach one another again. And they couldn't rely on other means. It seemed everyday another undersea cable snapped, and with no megacorps left to replace the internet cables and global cooperation an idea that never quite overcame the rising seas, those same seas would soon corrode the last links that traversed the world.

Aito turned on his universal translator. It made his voice tiny and odd, but she understood why he used it after she heard what he had to say.

"I've found a system that can unpack the nano bit, but we'll need a phantom, defragmented version. Then we can try to run a omnioscillation from your system. Otherwise, we'll need the capabilities of a processor with Sevaeli nano tech."

"Okay. Let's try the phantom image. Maybe we'll get lucky and get something today," Papahi said.

*

It took a week, but finally the omnioscillators completed their work. They had 5 images to show for it.

On the open line, Izan spoke first.

"What are those designs for?"

"Blueprints, really," Hiroto said.

"Blueprints," Izan agreed. "yeah except for that one maybe."

"They're not for the continuum engine," Aito said, disappointed.

"No," Papahi said. "That'd be too dangerous. Think of all the things that shouldn't run forever."

"I doubt we'd be able to find or even manufacture the parts for it anyway," Ava added. "Hmm, that last design is a pragmatic choice."

"For?" Hiroto asked.

"Us," Papahi answered. "It's a basic shuttle design."

"Built for evacuating," Ava said. "Zoom in on the bottom left corner?"

Papahi did. *Capacity: 34 (Tillers) — 437 (~Shlin~).*

"That's a small settlement. If a test run works, others can repeat it," Papahi said.

"And you intend to post this on Concourse?" Izan asked. "So . . . you want to build a spaceship?"

No one spoke. Papahi broke the silence.

"How else are we gonna reach Haven station and the settlements beyond? The air's worse every year. When's the last time you could spend two hours outside without a respirator?"

Izan didn't respond.

"And yes, I want to build a spaceship, Izan. You don't?"

*

Papahi thought she was making a joke until she heard it. After, she couldn't shake the feeling that this was the only way. She could accept that. What vexed her was that there might be one. Scores had chased a way and ended up in mass suicides, off of cliffs that would have given lemmings pause, at the bottom of the ocean, or destitute and more desperate than when they began. Some even called it the new SSIPS, the reckless abandon of imprudent routes to survival. She didn't want to think that she'd slipped into it, but to be honest she couldn't be sure. So instead she was resolute.

Izan agreed to write the post.

Around 3AM the call alert on her console chimed. She toggled the link next to her bed on.

"Pap, where are they supposed to send stuff?" Izan asked as soon as she answered. Damn good question. Even with parts and plans they'd need someone to build it and somewhere big enough to hold (*and eventually launch,* a quiet voice inside her added) it. In one place.

"Request the space first," she whispered. "You'll have to make it damn good, Izan." She cleared her throat. "Really. Damn good. Biblical. But... reasonable. Otherwise they won't take it seriously."

"Coño, is that all?"

"Just say what convinced you or you if you were more stubborn. What *did* convince you?"

"Hm. It's something, Pap. That's all. And I don't have to put on a VR hood and hook up an IV or waste away. It won't make me eat a bullet or believe someone's my savior. That's a better option than what I'm seeing out here."

Papahi didn't respond.

"You asked," he said.

"Read me what you have," she said.

They worked until sun up in New Zealand, and late afternoon in Montevideo, scrolling through the other posts on the site, looking for ones that inspired them and figuring out why, so they could apply it to their own, analyzing the most successful projects to find their commonalities. Izan reworked an entire paragraph from a 'Save the World. Build H748-KCs' post, which seemed appropriately industrious, and customized the design from a methane digester call to action. After Papahi read the final draft she couldn't get back to sleep.

She got out of bed and wheeled herself to the back storage unit, started counting oxygen tanks, trying to figure out how many she'd need to make it to the airport.

By midday the post saw a rush of activity. A user with the handle Freeloving volunteered a cluster of warehouses. Later the same day, FightfortheFuture volunteered his experience as a mechanical engineer, and RudeGirl88 £25 to the first 10 people to locate a part, big or small, on the list of materials that accompanied the blueprint. Over the next week, the rush grew into a steady surge.

Content to let Izan do what he enjoyed, Papahi listened as he ran down the list of all the people he'd been able to line up with the project's needs. After a solid 30 minutes about procurement channels, volunteer workers, and funders he stopped in midsentence.

"Can you fucking believe this?" Izan said.

"Believing in it is what makes it work," Papahi replied. Izan toggled his camera on. He had a beard now. It suited him. He shook his head. She knew what he was going to say.

"De veras?" he said.

It's not the first time he'd videoed in a "really?" She hoped he wouldn't have to for the next one.

*

Papahi arrived last. She'd spent three days trying to decide whether to take the exosuit or the chair. She'd brought the pair, which meant both she and the suit were exhausted by the time she arrived. After nearly 28 hours of travel and her extra battery near 30% she bounced along in a pedicab facing backwards so she could hold the chair's handle to keep it inside the trundle and in one piece.

The driver kept looking back, intermittently switching his focus from the gap in the seal where her arm poked though the velcro to her. She'd been surprised to find only electric bikes and pedicabs at the last station on the airport line. Apparently none of the other three drivers at the huge, empty station would chance a trip that far away from the O_2 booths.

The sky brightened to slate blue as the cab passed a comm tower and finally stopped in front of a long, rectangular warehouse that reminded Papahi of the midterm asthma care sites her mother used to work in after her grandfather sold the dive center. She hoped the Takas' penchant for planning ahead would serve them all well here.

She let go of the chair and resealed the velcro flap. Once she paid the driver and removed her bag from the trundle, she pulled the chair out, unfolded it, placed her bag in its seat and pushed the chair up to the huge door. She saw no other entrance. The exosuit battery at her wrist read 27%. Papahi pulled the door open one careful step at a time, holding and walking so as not to overtax the motors in the suit's shoulder. Once the opening was wide enough to accommodate the chair Papahi stopped and pushed it inside. It led the way as she stepped in and walked the door closed.

Inside, the warehouse was sectioned into portions. This room stretched easily 20 times the length of her space at home. It had a bare concrete floor, metal corrugated walls and two more huge doors on tracks, one in front of her, one to the right. Off in the back corner of the space stood a makeshift kitchen of stainless steel counters and an electric cooker next to a sink she could've bathed in. A refrigerator bigger than the pedicab faced her. A bank of bright lights shined straight down into the kitchen area, plunging the rest of the room into relative darkness.

"Hello?" she called.

"Unfair advantage." The voice came from her left. She knew it before she turned.

"Izan," she said smiling. As she came to a stop she found herself staring at his armpit. She laughed. Even in the exosuit she had to look up. That put him far past average height. He must have been nearly 2 meters tall. Papahi popped the release on her helmet. The acrid scent of chemical-conditioned air filled her nostrils.

"Oxygen tanks *and* a space suit? Unfair." He shook his head, smiled widely. "It's good to see you, Pap." He leaned down, embraced the exosuit. "Come on. Get outta that thing," he said, stepping back.

Papahi bent down and took her bag out of the chair's seat, squatted the suit down into it and locked the chair's hand brake. She hit the suit's release button. As she did Ivan knelt down on one knee.

Papahi wondered it he knew he did a tiny dance of expectation, rocking his shoulders slightly from side to side. She—was that a? She had to admit she giggled as the panels floated out and opened up on his face.

"Dah!" he said as he leaned in and grabbed gentle hold of her. Papahi felt warm flesh against her own as their arms touched, his hands slid across her neck as he embraced her. On the other side of her shirt he felt solid and smooth and soft. She closed her eyes. It had been far too long since she'd touched another person. She felt Ivan's stomach jump as a small noise escaped his mouth. His breath huffed across her back.

He pulled back, eyes wet.

"Hey, Papahi. Bienvenidos."

She heard foot steps hurry toward them.

"Papahi!" Hiroto yelled, but Ava beat him there. Aito not to be outdone cut in front of both of them, gave Papahi's shoulders a squeeze, the rest of her an open-mouthed "Ha!" and a kiss on the cheek before her deferred to Ava who grabbed her hand and joined Ivan on the floor, her head lower than his chest. Ava smelled of flowers though no one smelled of flowers anymore, not since Papahi's grandmother passed when she was a child.

"I thought you'd never get here." Ava rose a bit on her knee, touched her forehead to Papahi's.

"*Now* we can begin." Ava said. Behind her Hiroto beamed. Sick of waiting his turn he leaned in, pushing past Izan and hugged Papahi's right side warmly.

"Hello," he said next to her ear. His voice was deeper in person. He seemed much more like Aito's brother, in energy as much as their features. As Hiroto pulled back, the two now stood hip to hip. Looking at them all surrounding her, Papahi couldn't remember the last time she'd felt comfortable enough that it didn't matter that she couldn't see beyond what encircled her.

She felt safe enough to sleep right where she was.

"I . . .uh . . . hold on," she said and reengaged the panels. They lifted back into place. She stood the suit up and laid it down on the floor, pulled her padded gloves from their compartment, put them on.

Each of them watched keenly, but no one asked questions. They kept a close distance as she went through the ritual of emerging from the suit, setting the stability bar on the chair and climbing up. Papahi leaned back.

"Ok. When do we get started?"

*

She couldn't shake the feeling of surreality. No screen between them or microphones to funnel their voices was adjustment enough, but if the sight of the four of them in real life wasn't shocking enough, when Aito pulled the door on the right back and exposed thousands of shuttle parts and dozens of people going about the complicated business of organizing them in bins and chalked sections along the floor she could only blink and wait for an explanation. Izan spoke first.

"They were here when we got here. A couple of them have been filming everything and posting it to the Concourse. Aito and Hiroto have been leading the rest in the pick and place of it all. Inventory is still going on right, Aito?"

"Hai. It looks like we might even have a small surplus. I can't know how much of one yet. But it's a lot of parts, in a lot of different conditions."

"This is a basic shuttle?" Papahi said.

"Basic to whoever designed it, not us." Aito leaned in to her, and said softly.

"And those were your words, no?" He smiled, pulled back and spoke again to the group, "I've never heard of some of it, but it is remarkable. The safety measures, automated systems are extensive and—," he tipped his head to the right, "well thought out. As we organize, we're trying to reverse engineer the designer's thinking. I hope that will help with piloting though I would guess that it too will be heavily automated."

"It also makes their job," Hiroto said as he gestured to the people going about their work, "even more important. But it's a lot of parts."

"It's also a lot of languages," Aito interjected.

"Hai, we have three translators," Hiroto added. "Mine, Aito's and a person. We're not sure which is doing a better job."

"Yes, these are not common words, these parts, what to do with them. It's difficult," Aito said.

*

They ended up making up the words that were missing. The group held morning briefings on new words and what they meant along with an image dictionary, which led to more than one good laugh and the beginning of a fight.

In another two days, the inventory was complete. They had 117% of the necessary parts. The most essential units though were unique. They'd have to get a lot right the first time.

No one quite knew where to begin. They had blueprints but no instructions. To avoid blind alleys Aito suggested that they discuss the steps before they implemented them. The next challenge quickly became apparent. They had only requested the parts for a shuttle, not the heavy machinery to move its sections into place and hold them there while they were attached. Unless they planned on moving and housing hundreds of people to assemble it pyramid style they'd need a system of fulcrums, pulleys, levers, and ramps. That too would take some expertise and resources. Back Izan went to the site and so it went until it seemed they had every person who went to the Concourse adding something or another to the project, if only a comment or spare change.

A month later, they could move what they needed to.

"We'll be done by morning," Hiroto joked. Seventeen months later, they'd assembled 89% of the shuttle.

They built it together, piece by painstaking piece, sanded the rough edges until they glided and roughed the precious until it resisted in just the right place at the appropriate time. They turned their remnants whole and mended every broken thing into one of efficient beauty. Until the bindings themselves seemed as closed as skin. Until hope turned to pride and they sat exhausted before what they'd made and slept a deserved sleep, safe from the sky that would soon hold them.

Papahi woke to the heavy hush of three dozen people sleeping near her; a soft cough intermittently fluttered the pleasant curtain of sound. She closed her eyes and listened.

Hey eyelids opened slowly as she floated with the sound of it.

From a distance the shuttle's exterior looked textured, but Papahi knew they were maker's marks. Each person who'd had to custom fit a piece left one. They looked as distinct as the people who had fashioned a future from the leftovers and precious pieces of the world. They made the ship beautiful in a way she couldn't have anticipated—even here in the quiet of an unexpected hush.

In the morning the feeling lingered as folks began to rise and start their collective day. At the morning meeting, Aito had no new words to explain, just a question.

"What do we call it?"

"Ours."

Papahi didn't remember who had said it, didn't need to.

*

"What if they're still out there?" one of the assemblers, a short, red-headed man in all plaid, said to the woman opposite him.

Papahi overheard them as she logged off of the site.

"Who?" another chimed in from the seat he was fastening down to the main fuselage.

"You know who," a third responded.

"Costa Rica," a young woman interjected.

"No way it was terrestrial. That was the Qezzel, I'm telling you," another said.

"The Qezzel? They lost their planet," the first man said.

"Uh huh and *someone gave it back,*" came the response.

"It was sentry gunners, stationed out in the stratosphere, making sure they didn't have to share their resources with other humans," said the woman the first man had been talking to.

"I *said* it wasn't terrestrial."

"An EMP downed all those shuttles. What does that have to do with gunners?" the first man said.

"The sentries couldn't target them all so they hit the pulse," the woman opposite him responded.

"Costa Rica hasn't had an army in centuries."

"That's what they *want you* to think," the young woman said.

Papahi had heard versions of this conversation playing out as long as she could remember. Online or offline the chatter sounded the same.

The truth often depended on where you lived and always who you listened to.

Everyone knew that an nonnuclear electromagnetic pulse downed every aircraft in North America at the same moment. Answers to why and who varied. Papahi might have heard the truth once, but she'd be hard pressed to recognize it. Better then to listen to herself and she said there was no way of knowing so one had to forge on. She rolled back, away from the table and nodded at the assemblers talking as she passed by and they fastened a section of the shuttle onto one of the firewalls that separated each section from the next. Papahi rolled on to see what Ava and the guys were doing.

She found them in the sleeping quarters huddled around a monitor and VR set.

"Time for VR?" she asked as she approached. "Must be ahead of schedule."

Izan had the helmet on; his fingers worked furiously at the controller.

"It's the fairest way to decide," Hiroto said. "And it's not commercial VR. It's more like the immersion unit blueprint on the TIK speck, maybe even a little more advanced."

"You know tech specs now, Hiroto?"

"That's what Aito said," Hiroto offered just before he gave her the finger. "You're up after, Izan."

Papahi laughed as she returned the gesture. Good to see all this proximity hadn't changed him too much.

She did well on her turn, almost taking the top spot but Hiroto beat them all. He made sure they knew it. Then he did something that surprised her: made a dinner that had her going back for seconds. He even refilled their cups whenever he got up to top off his own. After, he bowed and found a quiet corner in the back to go through his exercise regimen.

Terea D. Johnson

"Aito," Ava said. "Your brother is . . . interesting."

"He's three different people. I just look like one of them," Aito responded.

Ava turned to him. "I like that."

*

The test flight played out differently than VR. In the first 10 minutes Hiroto discovered an overwhelming vertigo whenever he sat in the pilot's pod at the nose of the shuttle.

Papahi would pilot. True to his multitudinous form, Hiroto was the first to congratulate her, with real warmth in his eyes. After they'd all joined him in congratulating her, he took her aside. They stopped at the staircase next to a sleeping loft. He sat on the third step and turned to her.

"Was that a panic attack?" he asked.

"Yes," she said quietly.

"That's never happened before."

"Better to find out now."

"Not knowing is Buddha," he responded. "You'll do well. Best that Ava is the backup now. Which means—"

"You'll keep managing everyone. They love you Hiroto."

"Thank you, Papahi."

She waited for the snide remark to balance the moment, appreciated that Hiroto gave her nothing more than a nod.

*

She spent the morning of the launch in the bathroom. Papahi knew the ship would do most of the work, had been designed to do so. And she trusted Aito to check the details and Hiroto to have put the right people on the right job and reassign them when he thought it necessary. She trusted herself.

She didn't trust that competence and craft always sufficed. Reality could be a trickster. Perhaps here nerves were the trick. With that thought (and no small dose of acceptance) she drank a last sip of water and suited up for the walk to the ship.

Wearing helmets, respirators, gas masks and scarves, the assemblers, the tool and dye crew, inspectors, Ava, Hiroto, Aito and Izan pushed and pulled the shuttle out of the warehouse and out onto their makeshift tarmac. They could have used the main ramp's pulleys but it seemed to Papahi that they wanted to touch it, to have a last contact before they embarked on making good on their good works. When they'd cleared the distance markers Ava and Aito had measured and remeasured, all but the flight crew hung back.

The pilot sat at the head of the ship in a clear capsule that Ava had compared to the old gunner pods of the Qezzel. The pilot was part navigator in that a majority of her duties centered on confirming the shuttle's course readings and actions were correct. Essentially if all went well, the pilot was no more than the last redundancy in the system. The controls had limitations but within those limitations one could engage the ship's ability to maneuver should the primary automation fail. With six buttons and a joy stick she could right 97% of unforeseen issues. The remaining 2.8% lay outside of Earth technology's capability.

She got in the shuttle first, climbing the first three steps of the short ladder. Papahi placed her left foot on the fourth step, her right hand one rung above the left and leaned the suit back. She grabbed her gloves and hit the release. Once the panels opened, she climbed the last rungs of the ladder to pull herself free of the suit and lower herself down into the shuttle's interior. Cool air prickled the skin on her bare arms as she passed the lip of the entrance. The floors were cushioned, the same matte lead color of the rest of the interior; seats lined the sides. She leaned up against the seat closest fo the pilot's capsule waiting for each of them to enter. Ava would sit here in case she needed to take over.

Once they had gathered, Papahi thought of saying something, but the right words wouldn't come to her. Instead she squeezed each of their hands and began to hum a song with no melody. It filled the gap. They took their seats.

Papahi checked the safeties, while Aito ran a diagnostic. When she got the signal from Aito and her panel flashed green, she engaged the engines. The shuttle slowly pulled away from the warehouse. Rolling, it turned until it found an adequate stretch of free space. Papahi adjusted herself as the front end of the shuttle rose to an acute angle, pushing her further back in her seat. She initiated the launch sequence.

As she watched, the scene on the other side of the capsule shifted. First she saw the warehouse and the heads of the ground crew cheering, filming, crying, then just the tip of the comm tower, then the bright glare of the sky. Then speed, and streaks of color.

Change happened right then. They did not see the last of that world, the one that they had never been able to escape, only felt an echo of its demise as they pushed past the last tethers of gravity and experience. After all the thrust and crush of their work, the fire of their refusal to die quietly, separated from one another, they rocketed up through the thin atmosphere and into space proper.

Papahi cut their speed and engaged the jets that would maintain the vessel's equilibrium. Her eyes filled with tears as she turned and looked at where they'd come from, looked out at what there they might yet go.

She saw only possibility, and then a second later, light.

That was the mercy.

Papahi died instantly, the very nanosecond that Haven's sentry shot pierced that shuttle's pilot pod. The firewall held and the shuttle sections sealed just as quickly as they had been designed to. The 'chute and shields engaged.

All of it, the parts and people, both dead and alive, hurtled back to Earth. Again cut off from one another, but protected from all but gravity.

*

Ours ended its maiden voyage off the coast of Madagascar. It plunged into the sea before rocketing back up to the surface, driven by its rescue propulsion. The sections that held Aito, Hiroto, Izan, and Ava survived the crash. The rest of Ours sunk into the fathoms. The four friends worked together over the course of days to struggle to solid ground. They stayed there until the hurt went hard and they could move without tearing it open.

They'd forgotten that people were watching.

Besides them, there was only other person who

existed in their world. And she had disappeared with their dream.

*

The next time, people came to them. Because those people had come to understand. They now knew that they didn't have the luxury of getting over, and no longer had the hope of getting out. But the fire'd been lit. The whole world that still lived in the real world saw what they had done and what they almost did. A few people saw it in real time, but most through countless views of the footage that Aito couldn't look at once, that Ava committed to memory, that the others learned to avoid.

Those people, the ones who craved for better, they'd have to get through it. There was no other way. They came to the group with their want and asked that they shape it, give it a voice and a vehicle so that they might replace their longing with life.

Izan stayed offline. Now that the four of them lived together he said there was no need when he said anything at all.

Aito and Hiroto took short walks with him and tried to trade Japanese for Spanish, his pain for their patience. Hiroto seemed to have cultivated more in the quiet hours he spent drawing plans of what he'd like to see in the world. Aito learned to build a guitar and then to play one. All of them learned to stay out of Ava's studio.

Ava couldn't bear the thought of building another ship though she also understood that they were quickly reaching a time when they'd need a spaceship or something like it just to travel. She missed Antarctica's mild springs and though she didn't want to leave her friends she thought one day she might convince them to spend a season there. So the day might come when they'd make something quite like Ours. But the thought of going through it all again, this time without Papahi sent her to bed. She wouldn't succumb to despair, but she also couldn't go back down that particular road; in her heart, and she suspected her head, she'd end up at the same place. So Ava went back to the only place she'd seen glimmers of a future she might want to live. She scoured buildabetter.world for something she couldn't quite articulate.

She found a woman from Texas with an impassioned post filled with Clems and long walks in the open air, as well as the design for something called an H748-KC, a reformer, apparently a terraformer built for Earth to replenish the atmosphere.

She read on, read up, and readied herself to take another plunge. Then she worked to bring the fellas on board.

They would need a series of the reformers to have any chance at success. They didn't have a climate scientist among them. Ironically most of them had fled with everyone else of means, but there were three of the KCs in operation now, all built by or traded for by the woman who customized the original into existence, the 'C' in 'KC' the Clem who enabled long, lazy walks to get some breathable air. The original poster, Darla didn't know what had happened to the engineer. When Ava pressed her for more info, she wrote that the KC worked and they had the design, what more really mattered? She had a point.

*

Six months after the first round of KCs went online, a site scout found a climate scientist to evaluate the viable tropospheric units emitted by both the original and new KCs. After, Izan had to assure the man they had not gone to the great trouble of faking such results, having no idea how to do so. The guy wouldn't leave after that. So they put him to work, one of the many new faces buzzing around that work area and the next six sites Ava visited. She and each of the guys had eight now. Next month, they'd train others to take on the next round of builds.

They worked until it became life and found the satisfaction in that. Ava would sometimes accompany Izan's cheeky ballads to Hiroto's dedication to calisthenics just to hear Aito laugh so hard he snorted. They lived this way for years.

When they could stay out all night and dance in the open air, they knew the tide had turned even if the water kept rising. When other people could do it in pockets all over, the water seemed less mighty because they too had might. They could change might to will; there was no greater metamorphosis than that.

*

Ours, or rather its replica Ours Too, had a second flight, a voyage around the world to visit the assemblers, donors, engineers, supporters and recipients of their second chance. Ava piloted. If anything she looked even smaller in the pilot's pod than Papahi had, but she'd lost none of the aptitude or reaction time that a shaky launch or voyage would have shown.

In the intermittent years she'd learned to pilot three classes of starfarer. Coming to her calling late in life only made her that much more revered—now as the white-haired maverick slicing through clouds and space dust alike. These days Izan called her Legendary when they met for dinner. She'd learned to smile and accept a third glass of wine rather than try to hush him.

Izan joined her on that second trip, as did Aito and Hiroto. They stopped in Antarctica and over Tonga's grave too.

After, Ava centered Ours over the shipyard where mechanics waited to fortify it for its next trip, back out toward Haven to remind those requesting a return where things stood, and what they would no longer fall for.

Ava brought the ship down gently as a shed skin floating to the ground.

Papahi, the indestructible bit of energy that defined her, watched.

That's what they believed, the ones who had made it to that moment. And so it was.

ABOUT THE AUTHOR

Tenea D. Johnson's short work appears in anthologies like *Mothership: Tales from Afrofuturism and Beyond*, *Sycorax's Daughters, and Blue and Gray: Ghost Stories from the Civil War*. Her musical stories were heard at venues including The Public Theater and The Knitting Factory. Tenea also wrote a poetry and prose collection, *Starting Friction*. Her debut novel, *Smoketown,* won the Parallax Award. *R/evolution*, the first book in the Revolution series (which includes the novel, *Evolution*), also received an honorable mention that year. She is the founder of Progress By Design. Her virtual home is teneadjohnson.com.
Stop by anytime.

Made in the USA
Columbia, SC
30 June 2020